Realistic Fiction

# In the Shade of the Níspero Tree

YEARLING BOOKS are designed especially to entertain and enlighten young people. Patricia Reilly Giff, consultant to this series, received her bachelor's degree from Marymount College and a master's degree in history from St. John's University. She holds a Professional Diploma in Reading and a Doctorate of Humane Letters from Hofstra University. She was a teacher and reading consultant for many years, and is the author of numerous books for young readers.

# In the Shade of the Níspero Tree

Carmen T. Bernier-Grand

A Yearling Book

ACKNOWLEDGMENTS

*Mil gracias* to my Ponceño driver, Fernando A. Comulada, and to all of you who helped me with *marrayos*, photos, marshmallow weddings, songs, poems, sandalwood fans, submissions, art, moral support, editorial advice, and so many years of critiques!

*The children's poems used in the carnival contest were written by Erica María Marrero and Michael Antonio Marrero and appear here courtesy of Dr. Sonia Cintrón Marrero.*

*Excerpts of "Danza negra" by Luis Palés Matos appear courtesy of Ana Mercedes Palés.*

Published by
Dell Yearling
an imprint of
Random House Children's Books
a division of Random House, Inc.
1540 Broadway
New York, New York 10036

**Visit us on the Web! www.randomhouse.com/kids**

**Educators and librarians, for a variety of teaching tools, visit us at www.randomhouse.com/teachers**

ISBN: 0-440-41660-4

Reprinted by arrangement with Orchard Books, a Grolier Company

Printed in the United States of America

February 2001

10 9 8 7 6 5 4 3 2 1

OPM

*T*o Eloise Jarvis McGraw with love,
admiration, and gratitude for her
encouragement, not just to me but
also to other writers

Mami gave me the light pink envelope to open because it said: *"Señorita Teresa Giraux y familia."* *Caramba,* that sure made me feel special!

Inside was my teacher's wedding invitation. The card had two beautiful pink hearts overlapping each other. I opened it and read it slowly, because, even though I was at the beginning of fourth grade, I couldn't read fast. But I read it at least seven times.

*Sr. y Sra. Calixto Bocachica*
*y*
*Sr. y Sra. José Miranda*
*tienen el placer de invitarles a la boda*
*de sus hijos*

*Isabel*
*y*
*Carlos*

*Sábado, 7 de octubre de 1961*
*8:00 P.M.*
*Catedral de Nuestra Señora de la Guadalupe*
*Ponce, Puerto Rico*

Mami and Papi read it over my shoulders.

"How special!" Papi said, touching my cheek with the back of his hand.

"I'd better get busy." Mami turned around and headed toward the sewing room. "You'll need a new dress for that wedding."

Mami wanted me to be well dressed for *every* occasion. Sometimes I liked it; other times I didn't. When Ana wore those cute outfits she bought at Felipe García, I wanted to buy them too. Mami always said no. Too cheap! But when I visited Ana, I wore her clothes and she wore mine. We were the same size. Still, Mami made beautiful dresses, and I wanted to wear a new one to Miss Bocachica's wedding.

Papi followed Mami to the sewing room, but I stayed in the hallway, opening and closing the overlapping hearts. I read the wedding date one more time and checked it with the calendar by the phone. I counted the days to the wedding. Three weeks! Too long to wait.

I picked up the phone to call Ana and see if she'd received an invitation too. Miss Bocachica had called Mami earlier in the week to say that she was inviting Ana and me and our families to her wedding, but that she couldn't invite the whole class and their families. So she wanted us to keep the invitation a secret.

Ana's phone rang and rang. Nobody answered it. I hung up and read her phone number written on the wall. Yes, I'd dialed the right number, 2342. The 3 looked like an *E* because I'd written it in first grade when I used to write the three backward.

I dialed once more and counted the rings. Twenty-five of them. I hung up and waited, closing and opening the invitation. I was about to dial again when I saw Mami half closing the sewing-room door, which meant that she and Papi wanted to talk about something they didn't want me to hear.

I tiptoed to the door and peeked through the opening. Mami had her back to me—her long, black, straight hair clasped as always with a metal barrette. She unfolded a large piece of lilac taffeta, and my heart filled with envy. That fabric wasn't for my dress; it was for a dress for a girl who went to La Academia de Niñas.

"I don't get it, Dolores." Papi threw his hands up. "I just don't understand why you insist on taking Teresa out of Rafael Cordero School when she's doing fine there."

My stomach coiled up, then sprung down into the hollow, dark space in my belly. I liked Cordero and didn't want to go anywhere else.

I moved closer.

"Listen, Ramón," Mami said, pinning a pattern to the fabric. "This is our daughter's future. And let me say it one more time in case you didn't hear it before. Doña Carlota says La Academia is giving half scholarships for people like us this year."

"'For people like us'!" Papi yelled. "See how those people speak?"

"Ramón, those were not exactly her words."

"But that's the way those snobs speak."

Doña Carlota was the mother of the girl Mami had

been sewing the dress for. I hadn't met them, but they were of *la sociedad,* high-society people.

For a moment, I thought of myself as an Academia girl with a freshly pressed uniform, my hair styled just right, an expensive watch on my wrist.

Mami tapped the scissors on the table, shaking my thoughts away. "You need to leave your prejudices behind, Ramón. Think about your daughter's future."

Papi glanced toward the door. I pressed my back against the wall for him not to see me. "I *am* thinking about my daughter's future, and I know that at Cordero she's getting an excellent education. Come on, Dolores, you cannot ask for a better teacher than Isabel Bocachica."

"Ramón, be realistic. Isabel is marrying a soldier. Who knows! She might move."

I shook my head. The thought of Miss Bocachica moving hadn't crossed my mind. I didn't think she could do that, not after being our teacher for almost four years—five for Ana and the others because they went to kindergarten, and I didn't.

I tried to listen to Papi and Mami, but a car with a loudspeaker advertising La Gloria shoe store was passing by slowly.

*"TUS PIES EN LA TIERRA*
*TUS ZAPATOS EN LA GLORIA"*

"KEEP YOUR FEET ON THE GROUND
BUY YOUR SHOES FROM LA GLORIA"

~~~
4

I sat on the floor remembering how Mami had told me that she'd wanted to send me to La Academia in kindergarten. We couldn't afford it, and kindergarten wasn't a requirement, so I stayed home that year. From first grade on, children had to be in school. When first grade came, Mami tried again to enroll me in La Academia. Still, we couldn't afford it, and I ended up at Cordero.

Now I laughed, because I'd cried on my first day at Cordero. I had cried because Mami had cried, maybe because she hadn't wanted me to go to Cordero. That first day, it got to be hard for her and me to pull away from each other. After she'd finally left, Miss Bocachica held my hand with her soft, brown hand and sat me on the piano bench while she played and sang *"Muñequita linda,"* a song about a doll with golden hair, pearly teeth, and ruby lips. She sang the song to me, the only blonde in the whole class.

I cried throughout the song while the other children, sitting on the floor, stared at me. A girl with long, curly ponytails like black poodle ears stood up and offered me a handkerchief embroidered with Little Red Riding Hood and the wolf. It was so pretty that I didn't use it. When I tried to return it, she said, "Keep it."

That girl was Ana. That same day she called me "Tere," and we became best friends.

༄

The car with the loudspeaker finally moved on, and I heard Papi say, "Come on, Dolores, Teresa isn't like those Academia girls."

"That's the whole point, Ramón, that she's not like them and that she should be."

"Why?"

"Because if we want her to be successful in life, she has to be like them."

"I don't get it. Why can't she be like Ana, for example?"

"Ana is a very nice girl, but let's face it, Ramón. Ana can never be of *la sociedad*."

"Of *la sociedad*, as in high society?" Papi said jokingly. "Or of *la suciedad*, as in dirt?"

"Ramón, that's not funny!"

"Sorry," Papi went on. "But we're not of high society either, and I'm glad we aren't."

I knew that to be in *la sociedad* we had to have a lot of money. Other than that, I didn't know what else it took to be in it. Mami had said it as if it was a good thing to be, a very important thing to be.

I wondered why Ana could never be of *la sociedad*. Her parents didn't have much money. We had more than they did, but not much. Yet Mami seemed to think that we could be in high society, and Ana couldn't. It was as if something was wrong with Ana. But what could that be?

"Ramón," Mami said. "I just want Teresa to have the opportunities I once had."

"Well, I don't. I prefer to see her growing up among simple people like the ones who go to Cordero."

"*¡Ajá!*" Mami threw the scissors on the table and

placed her hands on her hips. "And how would you feel if she marries one of those boys?"

"Ha! And you tell me that I have prejudices! Dolores, we'd be lucky if Teresa marries one of those boys."

I stood up and leaned over to see Papi. He took a comb out of his coveralls pocket and began to comb his blondish hair. It wasn't any longer than the hair on his arms, so he didn't have to comb it. But he combed it a lot when he was upset.

I saw no reason for them to be upset. I knew Mami was worried just because I'd told her about my school friend Cesar and me. We'd curled *gongolí* worms around our fingers and said to each other "i do." We were just playing. But when I told Mami, she frowned and asked if we'd kissed. I told her that we didn't, and she sighed.

"Anyway, Dolores, Teresa is way too young for us to be thinking about her getting married."

"She is too young to get married, but she is not too young to start getting acquainted with high-society people."

"There you go again!"

"Ramón, I just want the best for Teresa."

"The best doesn't have to be La Academia, and I can't afford it anyway."

"But there are half scholarships, and Doña Carlota says—"

Papi plunked his hands on his head. "Doña Carlota says, Doña Carlota says—"

Mami raised her voice. "Doña Carlota says that if I do a good job with this dress, she'll hire me to make her girl's carnival gown, and I can always sew for more people."

"Crazy. Sew. Sew. Day and night." Papi's voice was really loud.

I felt like running into my closet and hiding there until they calmed down. But they were talking about me. I stayed, watching Papi take deep breaths and stare out toward the Sol de Borinquen, the bakery across the street. Don Felipe was baking *mallorcas* over there, and the sweet smell of those bread rolls came in through the window.

Papi moved away from the window. "We should ask Teresa which school she wants to go to."

I gulped and pressed my back against the wall. I could have run to my bedroom without being seen, but I stayed there, waiting for them to come for me. When they didn't, I peeked in again.

Mami picked up the scissors. Then she looked toward the door—right at me.

I walked into the room, embarrassed because they'd caught me eavesdropping. But they didn't seem to care.

"Teresa," Papi asked, "how would you like to go to La Academia de Niñas?"

I had no idea what to say. I wanted to know what it was like inside La Academia, and how it felt to be friends with those girls. But if I went there, I wouldn't see Ana as much.

"Can Ana go to La Academia too?"

"No," Mami snickered. "Of course not."

"Why not? Is it because she can never be a high-society girl?"

Papi looked at Mami, and Mami lowered her eyes the same way I did when I knew I did something wrong.

"Teresa," Papi said, after staring at Mami for a while, "why don't you think about what school you want to go to? You don't have to tell us tonight or tomorrow. Take your time."

I wanted to say that I'd decided already, that if Ana couldn't go to La Academia, I didn't want to go either. But Mami jumped in. "Not too much time. La Academia started two weeks ago, and I don't want her to be behind."

She placed her hand on Papi's shoulder. "Ramón, don't worry about the money. I've saved fifty dollars for some of the books and our share of the registration fee and the first month's tuition."

Papi shook his head. "Those people have money printed on their eyes."

I tried to imagine that—dollar signs popping out of people's eyeballs.

Papi kissed us and went back downstairs to his auto repair shop. I left after he did to call Ana, thinking that if I could find out what it really took to be in high society, we could both learn to be that way and we could go to La Academia together.

But Ana didn't answer the phone.

The next day, Sunday, I tried to persuade Mami to let me take Ana to Coamo, the town where my three grandparents lived. But Mami gave me the same excuse she'd always given me, "We need to take Abuelita to the cemetery, and she needs her privacy."

"¡Ay bendito! I never get to invite Ana."

Mami didn't let me invite Ana to the house when Abuelita came to visit either. I thought it was because Abuelita was toothless. Mami had bought her false teeth, but Abuelita hated them and never wore them.

As usual, it took us about an hour to get to Coamo. We went to Buelo and Buela's house first. They were Papi's parents—a chubby, short couple who looked more like twins than husband and wife. When Papi was growing up, they were poor. But later on, they did better, and Buelo tore down their old, wood house and built a modern, concrete block one.

As soon as we got there, Buelo asked me if I wanted to go to pump gas at his Shell station. I said yes, excited.

But Buela glanced at Mami, then told Buelo, "It's a sin to pump gas on a Sunday."

Buelo answered, "What is a sin is to leave people stranded without gas—even on Sunday."

It really wasn't pumping gas on Sunday that Buela worried about. She and Mami were really worried about what Abuelita would say when she smelled the gas on my clothes.

Still, I got to pump gas for two cars. Soon it got boring because nobody else came, and we returned to the house. We ate lunch. Then Mami, Papi, and I went to visit Abuelita.

She was waiting for us, sitting on a rocking chair in the veranda that went all around her wood house. This used to be a hacienda house, the biggest in a rundown neighborhood. All the houses were made out of unpainted wood. They had rusted zinc roofs and most stood on stilts.

A jukebox in a nearby bar played loudly:

> *"Yo la quise, muchachos, y la quiero,*
> "I loved her, guys, and I love her,
>
> *y ya jamás yo la podré olvidar.*
> and I won't ever be able to forget her.
>
> *Yo me emborracho por ella,*
> I get drunk because of her,
>
> *y ella quien sabe qué hará."*
> and who knows what she's doing."

"This neighborhood!" Mami shook her head. "Teresa, you go straight inside."

When I got to the veranda, Abuelita stood up,

gave me one of her squeeze hugs, and complained, "You smell like gasoline, and you're skinnier. I'm telling you, being skinny is a sign of poverty."

I shrugged.

She greeted Mami and Papi with kisses and hugs too. They followed her, and I followed them. The wood floor creaked as we walked through the living room that still had the same antique mahogany furniture Mami grew up with. The brocade upholstery was ripped and the paint was chipped, and I wondered why Abuelita didn't throw them away.

Before I entered the dining room, I stopped to see myself in the console mirror that began at a low table and went all the way up to the high ceiling. I didn't look skinny, at least not as skinny as Linda, another school friend. I didn't look poor either. I held my dress to the side and bowed to myself, looking at my white organza apron. Mami had painted on it a windmill and two Dutch girls wearing clogs. I wished I could have a pair of those clogs to go with my dress.

Abuelita's dining-room table could have seated all seven of her children. All of them except Mami "had gone to find fortune in the United States." Abuelita was saying that when I walked in.

Mami nodded. "They're doing very well there."

"In New York?" Papi snickered. "Puerto Ricans don't do well in New York."

I agreed. I liked it when my uncles sent photos of my little cousins playing in the snow. Yet Cesar had told me that the snow in New York turned black and ugly and that the whole city got as cold as a freezer. I couldn't live in a freezer, and I wondered why my uncles didn't move back to warm Puerto Rico.

"Ah, but my Edgardo lives in Queens!" Abuelita told Papi.

Papi shrugged, but Abuelita didn't notice. Staring at the soup Buela had sent her, she added, "I don't need charity." She said that whenever Buela sent her food.

I watched Abuelita eat at the table set with a clean, but stained, embroidered linen tablecloth and chipped fine china. I wanted to tell her that Ana and I had been invited to Miss Bocachica's wedding. I began, "My friend An—" I stopped when Mami pinched me.

Mami had never told me that I couldn't talk about Ana in front of Abuelita, but she'd always interrupted me when I did, and changed the conversation. That made sense, because if Abuelita knew I had a best friend, she'd want to meet her. And that was a problem because of Abuelita's teeth.

"What were you saying?" Abuelita asked.

"Nothing. Just that . . . " I peered out the dining-room window, toward the river, looking for something to say. "I . . . just want you to tell me about El Jacho so I can tell my friends."

The wrinkles around Abuelita's mouth disappeared with a toothless smile. "Dolores and the boys liked to go fishing on the river. I didn't want them to go, you know, because fishing is not for girls, and she and the boys could drown. I told them that if they went to the river, El Jacho would come at night."

"And it came!" Mami opened her dark brown eyes as if still scared. "At night, we looked out to the river, and we saw the snake called El Jacho with many tongues of fire coming out from every place of its body. Some days its body was short, but other days—especially on the days when we'd gone to the river because it had a lot of fish—El Jacho got very long."

Mami spoke in a spooky voice. "Sometimes one of those tongues broke apart from the rest and came our way. Closer. Closer. When we saw it coming up the stairs, we ran to bed and covered ourselves from head to toe."

Abuelita laughed. "I sneaked under their beds and shook them."

"We thought it was El Jacho!" Mami cried. "My bed shook for a long time, but it was because *I* was shaking all over."

Mami and Abuelita held hands and laughed. I loved seeing them having fun.

"It wasn't until . . . " Mami stopped to laugh again. "It wasn't until I was big that I figured out that El Jacho wasn't anything else but fishermen with lanterns, and that the tongue of fire that came to our house was the lantern of a fisherman who came to sell us fish."

Abuelita shook her head. "Those were the good old days."

The wrinkles on her face sagged, matching the sadness of her black mourning dress. She always wore black because she was a widow—twice—and widows wore black the rest of their lives. I touched her arm to make her happy and ended up jiggling the soft, flappy skin under her arm. It was like a white, soft pillow that, if given to me, I'd have taken everywhere.

"We used to own all this, you know, Teresa?"

I nodded. I'd heard this many times from Abuelita.

"All this from here to all the way down to the river was ours." She stretched out her arm across the land. "We were in high society, and we had prestigious friends, and Dolores wore pretty dresses and went to parties at El Casino."

Abuelita had finished eating, but she swallowed hard, her hand on the big, round, gold medal of the Virgin Mary that hung from a thick chain, the only piece of jewelry she wore besides the seven silver bracelets that represented her children. "Then the hurricane San Ciprián came and razed everything, including my Florencio. *¡Ay, mi Florencio!*"

This was the beginning of what Papi called "Abuelita's Sunday ritual." I didn't look at him. If I did, we'd crack up laughing, and Abuelita wouldn't like it.

Abuelita first married Abuelito Florencio, Mami's father. During the hurricane, a piece of zinc that blew off from the roof hit him and killed him. A few years later, she married Abuelito's brother, Tío Cansio. He died *de repente*. For a while I thought *de repente* was some terrible sickness. Many people died *de repente*. People would ask, "What did he die of?" and the answer usually was, "*De repente*." But *de repente* meant "suddenly." It also meant that they didn't know what the person had died of. Anyway, Abuelito's brother died *de repente*.

After Abuelita finished eating, we took her to the cemetery. I liked the Coamo cemetery because it had many mausoleums, kind of like little castles with chapels where wealthy families buried their people. Abuelito and Tío Cansio were not buried in those. Their tombs just had concrete grave markers flat on the ground. Yet that was better than being buried in the little niches in the collapsing far end wall of the cemetery.

As usual, Abuelita swept Abuelito's grave marker, changed the flowers in the vase, prayed the whole rosary, and cried, "*¡Ay, mi Florencio!* I love you."

She blew him a kiss and moved to the next grave marker, Abuelito's brother's. She swept it, changed the flowers, prayed another rosary, and cried, "*¡Ay, mi Cansio!* I love you so much."

I bit my tongue, trying not to laugh. But I didn't talk about it until we had left Abuelita at her house, and we were on our way to Ponce.

"If Abuelita could choose today, who do you think she'd want to marry, Abuelito or Tío Cansio?"

"She'd choose Florencio," Papi answered, "because he was the member of El Casino."

"Ramón!" Mami scolded, smiling.

"Why wasn't Abuelito's brother a member of El Casino?" I asked.

Mami unfastened the barrette that held her straight, black hair into a ponytail. She combed her hair with her hand and clasped it with the barrette again. "Teresa, when the hurricane flood drowned all our cows and chickens, and the wind uprooted all our coffee plants, we were left with nothing. Tío Cansio married your Abuelita to help her, but it was hard to feed all seven of us. We couldn't return to El Casino because of its expensive membership fee."

"Were you a member of El Casino, Papi?"

"Never." He hit the steering wheel. "I hated that place! I went once with my godmother and had a terrible time."

He glanced at me in the rear-view mirror. "They got a group of us to play a game like hot potato but with a baseball. They told us that whenever the music stopped, whoever had the ball could keep it. I wanted that ball badly . . . "

He paused, but I could tell that the memory was still vivid in his mind.

"Did you get the ball?" I asked.

He nodded. "*Ajá,* when the music stopped, I had it in my hands. But a boy took it from me. My godmother argued that I'd won the ball, but they gave it to him just because he came from a wealthy family."

"That was your perception, Ramón. But maybe that wasn't the reason."

"That was the reason, and because of that I never set foot in that place again."

~~~~
*17*

"Ah," Mami said, "but it's good to rub elbows with high-society people."

"Why?" I asked, feeling that I wouldn't want to rub elbows with the boy or the person who took away the ball from Papi.

Mami answered, "Because they are distinguished and everybody respects them."

I couldn't understand that. Why would anybody respect a person who is not fair?

"Distinguished?" Papi said. "*¡Jaitones!* That's what they are. Snobs! They think they're superior just because they're whiter and have money."

"Ramón Giraux, there's nothing wrong with being white," Mami, who was much whiter than Papi, said. "And let me tell you, not everybody who is in high society is snobbish. I wasn't."

"That's what you think!"

"Ramón, you didn't know me then." Mami turned to me. "Teresa, don't listen to your father. He wasn't in high society. I was . . . and I wish I could still be."

"You cannot know much about it," Papi said, driving past a bright red *flamboyan* tree. "Because you were not in high society for that long."

"I was until I was ten, Ramón, enough to have a good taste of it." Mami turned to me again. "Teresa, believe me, you will have a better life if you grow up among high-society people, like the ones who go to La Academia. You will learn their ways, and they will fall in love with you!"

I leaned forward. "Did somebody in high society fall in love with you?"

Papi hit the steering wheel. "Good question! Why didn't you marry somebody from high society? You and your mother would have been happier."

"Ramón, I married you—against my mother's wishes—because I love you."

"Against Abuelita's wishes?"

"Yes, Teresa," Papi said. "Abuelita didn't like me because I wasn't in high society."

"But she adores you now, Ramón. And she'd always known that, with a little sacrifice, you and your parents could have been members of El Casino. But no, because you people are so stubborn!"

"That would have been foolish," Papi said. "Not only did I hate that place, but we had other priorities. Termites were destroying our house, and we had to replace it." Papi paused to pay attention to a car passing ours, then he said, "If there had been any extra money, my parents would have sent me to college, but there was no money to spare."

That I knew! Hoping to go to the Catholic University of Puerto Rico, Papi had moved to Ponce, where the campus was. But he couldn't afford the tuition, and he ended up working as a mechanic—first for somebody else, then by himself.

I thought that Papi was too old to be a student, but I asked him, "Do you still want to go to college?"

"No, my princess, I love what I do. Besides, your studies are my priority now."

"Then send her to La Academia!"

"No need for that, Dolores."

"There is a need." Mami made a face. "Teresa,

what your father doesn't understand is that, as a person educated among high-society people, his daughter may enter a jewelry store or a bank, they'll see her all dressed up and with fine manners, and they'll treat her like a queen." Mami danced her hands in a delicate way. "She'll tell them who she knows, and if she has a problem, they'll help her."

"Help her? Tell me, Dolores, did they help you when Cansio died and you were starving?"

"I never starved, Ramón. Never."

"Not because they helped you, but because I helped you."

"All right, rub it in. Is that why you married me, to take me out of poverty . . . because you pitied me?"

"Dolores, I married you because I fell in love with you. And because I love you, I work hard for you and Teresa to have what you need. But we don't need luxuries. And I don't want to rub in anything, but I resent when you forget that who helped you wasn't in high society."

"Let's stop this conversation, Ramón. Please, let's stop it!"

For a while, Mami peered out the passenger window, something she'd told me a million times not to do because it makes you carsick.

Then Papi turned the radio on.

*"¡Vida! Si tuviera cuatro vidas, cuatro vidas*
*serían para tí."*
"Life! If I had four lives, the four lives
would be for you."

~~~~~
20

This was my parents' song. Papi joined the radio singer. *"¡Alma! Si te llevas mi alma contento moriría por tí."* "Soul! If you take my soul, I would happily die for you." He smiled, and peered at Mami out of the corner of his eye.

Mami turned to face him, her eyes shining as much as her jet-black earrings. She let him finish the next verse, then joined him. *"¡Corazón! Si mi corazón te llevas, mi alma, mi vida, y mi ser—si tuviera cuatro vidas, cuatro vidas serían para tí."* "Heart! If you take my heart, my soul, my life, and my being—if I had four lives, the four lives would be for you."

# 3

*I* lived on the second floor of a two-story building, and I liked to pretend that I lived in a castle. But on the first floor, Papi had his auto repair shop. Instead of having royal horses, we had cars that wouldn't start. Instead of having a king, I had a father who had just rolled out from under one of those cars—his face freckled with grease, his hands so completely covered with grease that they looked like black gloves.

I asked him for his blessing as I did every day before I left, and he said, "May God bless you, my princess, and have fun in school." He blew me a kiss and I blew him one back.

On the way to school, which was only four blocks away, I saw bread and fruit vendors pushing their brightly colored wooden carts, *público* cars dropping and picking up passengers, and a welder sitting by a corner stand. As women passed by, he repeated:

> *"Señora, Señora,*
> "Lady, lady,
>
> *le arreglamos la cartera;*
> we can fix your purse;

*le soldamos la olla;*
we can weld your pot;

*y le enderazamos la sombrilla."*
and we can straighten your umbrella."


Once when my umbrella broke, Mami paid this man to fix it. "It's cheaper than buying a new one," she'd said.

That Monday, I told myself that an Academia mother wouldn't pay a welder to fix her daughter's umbrella. She'd buy a new one instead.

Then I saw Ana, standing by the Cordero gate, waving Miss Bocachica's invitation.

She ran to me. "Did you get yours?"

"Yes, but we're not supposed to talk about it in school."

"I know." She unbuttoned the first two buttons of her shirt and slipped the invitation inside it.

We went through the school gate, arched by purple and orange *trinitaria* flowers, and into the hibiscus path. Then the bell rang, and we ran to be first in line. Other children lined up behind us, and Miss Bocachica came out. *"Buenos días por la mañana,"* she said. "Good morning in the morning."

She had on the light linen skirt and the pink blouse with white embroidered butterflies that I liked. Her long, wavy hair went down her back like a waterfall.

"I'll return your compositions today," she said,

walking to the front of the room after we'd all sat at our desks. "But first, let me read you this one. It has some misspelled words, but I love it."

I thought she was going to read one of Ana's poems. But to my surprise, she began to read *my* composition.

> "The *coquí* is a tree frog
> who sings all night and when it rains.
> He sings 'Kokee! Kokee!' when he's happy
> and 'Ko-kee-kee!' when he's unhappy."

"Kokee! Kokee!" Luis sang.

"Ko-kee-kee!" Cesar cried.

"Boys," Miss Bocachica said. "Let me finish."

She continued reading, making me feel really special!

> "The *coquí* is never a tadpole.
> He never has a tail.
> Because when he hatches from his egg,
> he has legs!"

"Who wrote it?" Ana asked when Miss Bocachica finished.

Miss Bocachica pointed at me. "I thought so," Ana said, and everybody applauded.

"Who told you so much about the *coquí*?" Miss Bocachica asked me.

"Abuelita."

"Good for her and for you!" Miss Bocachica said, handing me the composition.

The paper had three gold stars, an A-minus, and a note that said "Very interesting!"

"*¡Chévere!*" Ana said, taking a peek at it. "Neat!"

We spent most of the morning correcting our compositions. Miss Bocachica made me rewrite mine many times until it was perfect. Then she displayed it on the bulletin board.

After a lesson on long multiplication, everybody left for lunch—everybody but Ana, Miss Bocachica, and me. Ana lived too far to go home for lunch, so I usually stayed with her in school. Sometimes we helped Miss Bocachica in the classroom, but most of the time, Ana and I sat to eat in the shade of the *níspero* tree.

We loved it there. At lunchtime, everything got quiet. The stores were closed and many people took siestas. The only sounds around us were those of the leaves dancing with the occasional breeze and that of *nísperos* falling on the ground.

The air felt softer and cooler under the shiny green leaves on these tree branches that sometimes bowed when they heard us talk. It was here where we shared secrets, whispering them to each other as if they were prayers.

"I can hardly wait for the wedding," Ana whispered to me after we had eaten our sandwiches. She cleaned her hands on a paper napkin, then took the invitation out from under her shirt.

I laughed. "You kept it there all morning?"

Ana nodded.

"Didn't it tickle?"

~~~

"It did, Tere, but it also reminded me of that day."

I picked up two *nísperos* from the ground. "I wonder what Miss Bocachica's fiancé looks like."

"Handsome, I hope. I wonder if they kiss."

We giggled. Then I said, "Mami is making me a new dress for the wedding."

Ana lowered her head, then slipped the invitation inside her shirt again. I could tell she didn't have a new dress to wear. I wished I could offer her one of mine, but Mami didn't allow me to give Ana any of my new dresses.

I placed a *níspero* in Ana's hand. Her skin and the skin of the *níspero* were exactly the same shade of brown. But her skin was softer.

I peeled my *níspero* and took a bite, a sweet flavor I loved. Ana took a bite of hers. I could tell that she was enjoying it, because her eyes were as shiny and dark as the *níspero* seeds I now had in my hand.

"I cannot understand why the new supermarkets don't sell *nísperos*," I said.

"They sell them at La Plaza del Mercado," Ana reminded me. She paused, then added, "Maybe they don't sell them in the new stores because the people who go there don't like them."

I thought about it. La Plaza del Mercado was where the mountain people came to sell their goods. Mami didn't go there anymore because she said the place had the smell of chickens, cilantro, plantains. The new supermarkets didn't smell like that because they sold everything wrapped in plastic. Still, they didn't sell *nísperos*. They probably were not fancy enough for the supermarket customers.

I shrugged. They didn't know what they were missing.

〰

After school I asked Ana if she could come over to my house. She called her father; he gave the okay and we headed home.

"What should we play?" I asked her on the way.

"Hide-and-seek in your father's piles of tires."

I hated to play hide-and-seek with Ana in Papi's tires. When it was my turn to hide, Ana always found me because my light hair was easy to see. But when she hid, I couldn't find her.

"No, let's play fancy ladies."

"Tere, I want to play hide-and-seek."

"Well, I don't want to."

Ana stopped walking, and crossed her arms.

"Come on." I pulled her gently by the arm. "We can make jewels out of Papi's metal nuts and bolts."

Ana began to walk again.

When we got to the shop I told Papi about my *coquí* story. He congratulated me. Then I asked him if we could play in the bins of bolts and nuts, and he said, "Sure," with a smile.

For a while we pretended the metal nuts were rings in a very expensive store. I slipped a ring on each finger and curtsied, thinking about this year's carnival.

This year Ana and I could participate in the

carnival pageant. The first week in November each school would choose two fourth-grade girls with fairly good grades to compete for junior queen of Ponce. I wanted to compete, be queen, wear a gown and a crown!

I slipped on another ring and told Ana, "Let's go upstairs and make carnival gowns."

I tried to take Ana's hand. I couldn't. She also had metal nuts on her fingers. Laughing, we ran up without holding hands.

"Mami! Mami!" I called, until I found her in the sewing room. "Can we have fabric to make gowns?"

Mami said hi to Ana and gave me a hug. She peered at our fingers and smiled. "I don't have enough scraps, but you could make gowns out of newspaper."

"No!" I cried.

"Ah-ah, just wait, you'll like them." Mami cut a hole in the center of a newspaper page. "I made newspaper gowns when I was your age. That's how I learned to design clothes."

She put the page on me as if it were a shirt.

"I don't like it!" I complained, seeing myself in the mirror.

"Just wait." Mami taped up the sides of the newspaper, making pretty ballooned sleeves. Then she took a bunch of newspaper pages, taped them together, gathered them up, and taped them to the shirt.

I twirled around. "It does look like a gown!"

I paraded in the room while Mami made Ana's gown. For her, Mami had chosen the Sunday comics.

I almost complained that her gown was colorful and mine wasn't, but I changed my mind. Mine looked as if it had rhinestones!

"Pretty!" Ana said, looking at herself in the mirror. "I want to keep it forever."

Mami laughed, and Ana added, "You have the most beautiful teeth."

Mami's teeth were perfect. But I knew Ana had said that as a way to thank Mami.

"They're false teeth," Mami teased. "Do you want to see them out?"

Without waiting for Ana's answer, Mami pretended to pull them out. "They don't want to come out today. Teresa, help me."

I put my fingers full of nuts on Mami's teeth and pulled, laughing. "They are stuck!"

Ana came closer to help. But when she tried to stick her fingers in Mami's mouth, Mami moved back, closed her mouth, and shook her head.

Ana froze.

"Mami," I said, "why did you do that?"

"I'm sorry," Mami said sternly. "But it's not sanitary."

I looked at Ana's fingers, still full of nuts. "But . . . you let me put my hand in your mouth."

"Teresa, you're my daughter." Mami picked up the newspapers from the floor. "I probably have your germs, but Ana . . . " She bit her lip and took a deep breath. "Ana might get my germs. . . . You don't want to get my germs, do you, Ana?"

Ana shook her head.

~~~~

I agreed. I didn't want Ana to get sick.

"Come." Mami motioned her. "Let me make you a crown."

I could tell Mami was embarrassed because she'd hurt Ana's feelings. She had a lot of sewing to do, yet she made Ana a newspaper crown with pointy things and another for me. She also attached newspapers to the backs of our gowns to trail behind us, like magnificent trains.

I walked, looking back at my train. "I can be the Carnival Queen of Ponce! And Ana, you can be my princess."

"No—no, let Ana be queen."

Mami's urging voice told me that she was still trying to make Ana happy. I did, too, but I didn't want to be princess. "Couldn't we have two queens?"

"Sure," Mami said.

"I'll be the Queen of Ponce, and you can be the Queen of . . . Coamo!"

Ana shook her head. "I'll be the Queen of Puerto Rico."

"Okay," I said.

We paraded downstairs and pretended that the car Papi was fixing was our royal coach. He bowed as we passed by, then we went back up.

At the top of the stairs, we found wooden crates piled high.

"Your thrones, Your Majesties." Mami bowed.

*4*

*T*he next day, coming back from school, I noticed a
white Cadillac parked by Papi's shop. I thought he
had a fancy customer, so instead of stopping to tell
him about my day, I went straight upstairs.

At the top of the stairs, I found a woman wearing
a beehive hairdo. A girl stood by her.

"Is this your daughter?" the woman asked Mami,
who had her back to me.

Mami turned, peered at me, checked behind me
as if looking for somebody, and sighed. Combing my
curls down, she said, "Yes, this is Teresa. Teresa, this
is Doña Carlota, and this is her daughter Marisol."

The girl flashed me a smile. She had braces and,
to me, that was fancy! Marisol. The name fit her. *Mar
y sol*. Sea and sun. Sea in her aqua eyes. Sun on her
shiny red hair.

Mami pinched me lightly on the back of my arm, a
reminder that I had to say, *"Encantada.* Nice meeting
you." The words didn't come out because I didn't feel
fancy enough in front of these ladies. But Marisol was
peering at my curls and face as if I was the fancy one.
Her smile made me feel like the *muñequita linda* of
Miss Bocachica's song.

"Mama," she said, patting her mother's arm. "Could she come over to our house?"

"Not today, Marisol, because we need to go to Katrina's house."

Marisol made a face. "I don't want to go to Katrina's house."

"We have to." Marisol made another face, but she smiled when her mother added, "Dolores, maybe you can take Teresa with you when you come to our house to fit Marisol's dress."

"I will," Mami said, excited.

I was excited, too, because I wanted to know how this girl lived.

After that, Marisol and her mother said good-bye.

As soon as they were gone, Mami sighed again. "I thought you were coming from school with Ana. From now on, check with me before you bring her."

Mami went inside. But I stayed there—confused. Mami had always said anybody could come to our house whether they were invited or not. She said, "If I have to add more water to the soup for them to eat, I will. But everybody is invited." As long as Abuelita wasn't at our house, Mami had always welcomed Ana.

∽

A few days later we went to Marisol's house. She lived up on El Vigía. From the top of that hill, I could see the whole city of Ponce. My house. The cathedral. And way down at the bottom, Ana's house.

Mami parked in front of a big, Spanish-styled house with curved roof tiles. What a place! We went through the walkway, where Mami admired the huge, velvety red roses. Then she rang the bell.

I expected a maid to open the door, but Doña Carlota did. "¡*Adelante!* Come in."

Marisol came dashing down a set of curved stairs. She stopped at the bottom, between two huge vases with painted sugarcane flowers. She was wearing white jeans, a canary yellow blouse with spaghetti straps, and white sandals on very clean feet.

"*Hola,*" she said, giving me a braces-smile.

"*Hola.*" I felt like a baby in my organza apron dress. The bow on my back felt stupid. The bobby socks, the black patent-leather shoes with straps— my whole outfit felt stupid.

Marisol took my hand. "Come, I'll show you around."

It was customary to show the house, but I looked at Mami and Mami looked at Doña Carlota, who said, "It's okay."

Marisol showed me the living room, where we were not supposed to play. I wouldn't have liked to play in there anyway. It was a dark room—maybe because all the windows were shuttered—full of antique furniture from Marisol's great-great-grandmothers. Their photos hung on a wall. The grandmothers had spooky dark circles under their eyes.

But all the other rooms were sunny and cheery. The family room—I'd never heard of a family room— had wallpaper with peach-colored flowers matching *two* soft sofas, so different from our beige plastic one. They also had a big TV!

On the hallway walls there were framed hand fans—one of them had a painting of Spanish girls dancing. For a moment I wished Mami would take down the picture of the Sacred Heart of Jesus and hang up hand fans instead. That would have been a sin. If throwing away a piece of bread without kissing it was a sin, replacing a picture of Jesus with dancing girls had to be a big one.

"Are you Catholic?" I asked on our way upstairs.

"Yes. Why?"

"I've never seen you in church."

"We go to the eleven-thirty Mass."

"I see," I said. "We always go at ten."

We never went to the eleven-thirty Mass, because otherwise we would have arrived in Coamo too late to take Abuelita to the cemetery. Before I could explain this to Marisol, she opened the door to her bedroom.

It was a bedroom for a princess! She had a four-poster bed like Ana's, but Marisol's had a pink tulle canopy. The cotton bedspread had little rosebuds exactly the same as the ones on the wallpaper. The walls also had shelves and shelves of these perfect little dolls.

"What are they?"

"Ginny dolls."

A Ginny doll on roller skates. A ballerina Ginny doll. A bride Ginny doll.

"Would you like to play with them?"

"Sure."

I'd thought I was in heaven, and I was sure of it when Marisol took out a toy closet full of doll clothes. It even had hangers! For a while, I didn't say anything. I just undressed and dressed a Ginny with different outfits. A pink-and-white gingham dress with white pantaloons. A blue velvet dress with a hat, tights, black shoes, and purse. A furry pink coat, beret, and shoes. I didn't play with dolls anymore, but I wanted to have all of these.

Marisol just watched me. I could feel her eyes on my hair and, at one point, she pretended to be trying to reach out for a hanger, and she gently pulled on one of my curls. I couldn't understand why she did that. To me, her hair was prettier than mine. I should have been caressing hers, but it looked like the silky red thread on an embroidered tapestry that I wouldn't dare touch.

"Do you mind if I call you Tere?" she said.

That surprised me. Ana called me Tere too, but Ana was my best friend.

"Why do you want to call me that?" I asked.

Marisol shrugged. "It's shorter than Teresa, and it sounds friendlier. But if you don't like it . . . "

"No, I like it. I like it."

Calling me Tere meant to me that we were friends. I felt like jumping up and down. I had a fancy friend! But it would have been silly to show so much excitement.

I turned around to get another outfit, and I saw Marisol's open closet. She owned as many shoes as her Ginny dolls did: red shoes, pink shoes, tennis shoes, more sandals. *¡Ay bendito!* I only owned the black-patent leather pair I had on, my school loafers, and the dirty white tennis shoes I wore to play. At least I had them. Ana played wearing her school loafers. I thought Mami was right. I couldn't take Ana home when Marisol was visiting. Ana would feel out of place, and I didn't want her to feel that way.

Marisol also had many dresses and—one, two, three uniforms. That reminded me of something Mami had said. "Mami told me once that La Academia girls can't go shopping wearing their school uniforms. Is that true?"

"*Ajá*." Marisol nodded.

"Why?" I asked.

She shrugged. "My mother says it's because La Academia doesn't want to get a bad reputation if somebody catches us doing something wrong."

I couldn't imagine what they could do wrong. Steal? I didn't think La Academia girls had reasons to steal. They had everything.

If I went to La Academia, I could have some of these things. Mami wouldn't want me to look as if I had less than any of those girls. That I knew. But I couldn't go to La Academia without Ana. And I'd miss Miss Bocachica.

Doña Carlota called, interrupting my thoughts. We put away everything and ran to the family room, where Marisol tried on the dress Mami was making for her.

"Not much of a dress yet," Doña Carlota said, sitting on the love seat, smoking, and swinging her crossed leg. Mami didn't think it was proper for a woman to smoke, but Doña Carlota looked like a movie star.

"It isn't much of a dress yet because it's still pinned together. But it's going to be princess style, like the dresses Jacqueline Kennedy wears. Simple but elegant."

Mami sounded nervous. Doña Carlota hadn't hired her to make Marisol's carnival gown, but wanting to have a head start, Mami had designed it already.

Marisol was going to represent a *guanábana,* a green fruit, creamy white inside, so the gown Mami had designed would be in green velvet and creamy-colored tulle. I wished I could wear a gown like that. If I went to La Academia, maybe I could.

When we got ready to leave, Doña Carlota and Marisol walked us out. I felt bad about them seeing our seven-year-old car, but they didn't make any faces when they saw it.

"Come any time," Doña Carlota said, closing my door.

Marisol nodded, smiling, and Mami and I waved good-bye. Then Mami began to drive down the hill.

But I couldn't let go of all the fancy things I'd seen.

I sighed. "Mami, if I go to La Academia, I can have a gown like Marisol's?"

Mami put her hand on my shoulder. "Teresa, La Academia celebrates its carnival at El Escorial. We cannot go there because we're not members. But I'll tell you what. If you go to La Academia and you become queen, I'll make you a gown prettier than Marisol's."

That was a temptation, a *big* temptation.

*T*hat Saturday, while watching the *Mickey Mouse Club* on TV, I heard, "Ramón!"

I ran to the balcony and saw Don Toño parking his red-and-black taxi. Ana's mother waved at me from the front seat of the car and Ana from the backseat.

I ran to the stairs, turned around, ran to the living room, turned off the TV, and said really loud so Mami could hear me, "Ana and her parents are here!"

I slid down on the concrete handrail, jumped off, and rushed out to the street.

"*Caramba,* young lady," Papi was telling Ana. "You sure are beautiful."

I was glad Papi had said that. Ana always complained that people called her cute—never beautiful.

She did look beautiful with her hair in braids. Mami never let me braid mine because it made my hair look wiry.

"We came to steal Teresa for the rest of the weekend," Don Toño said, and I clapped.

Ana smiled. "We're going to have a marshmallow wedding."

Before I could ask what a marshmallow wedding was, Papi said, "A marshmallow wedding! I imagine that's an event Teresa can't miss. Teresa, call your mother . . . ah, here she comes."

"Well, what a surprise!" Mami said, coming down slowly.

I remembered that Mami didn't want Ana to come by surprise, but I didn't think more about it because Doña Monse said, "We came to invite Teresa to spend the rest of the weekend with us."

"No, Monse, not this weekend." Mami kept one foot on one step, the other foot on a lower step. "I need her here to try on the dress I'm making her for Miss Bocachica's wedding."

"But, Mami," I cried, "you're just cutting out the dress. I'll have plenty of time to try it on later. Let me go, please. I promise I'll stand still when I try it on."

"Look, tomorrow is Sunday, and we have to visit Buelo, Buela, and Abuelita."

"I visited them last week. I don't have to go this Sunday, too, do I? *¡Ay bendito!* Mami, let me go, please. Pleeease."

Mami had told me many times not to pressure her in front of other people, but it always worked. "Okay. Go get ready."

"Quickly!" Doña Monse held Ana's arm so she wouldn't follow me. "Toño needs to return to work."

I went up, packed quickly, and rushed down. I gave Mami a big kiss and hug for letting me go, kissed Papi, and went with Ana into the car.

I'd always thought it looked like church in there. The red plastic seats in the taxi were as hard as the benches in church. Don Toño had a plastic rosary dangling from the rear-view mirror, and a sign on the dashboard that said:

*DIOS ILUMINE NUESTRO CAMINO.*
GOD ILLUMINATE OUR PATH.

I was wearing shorts, and it was so hot that my thigh got stuck to the seat. I lifted my thigh and it made a sound like Scotch tape being pulled off from plastic. Ana and I laughed.

"What's a marshmallow wedding?" I asked her on the way to her house.

"We make the bride, groom, and bridesmaids out of marshmallows. We already bought a bunch of candies from Maruca."

I sighed, relieved she'd said that in the car. Mami didn't let me buy Maruca's candies. Though he sold American candies that were wrapped, she didn't think they were sanitary—maybe because Maruca never wore shoes.

"We also bought a cupcake to use as a wedding cake and food coloring to color the bridesmaids' dresses. Then we can eat them!"

I gasped. "Eat them? I can't eat Miss Bocachica!"

Don Toño laughed.

"We don't have to name the marshmallow bride Miss Bocachica," Ana said. "We can give the bride and groom other names. Then we can eat them."

At that moment I didn't care what Mami had said. Ana was my friend. And I thought we must be the same kind of people, because her father was a taxi driver and Papi was a mechanic. But as we drove into Ana's neighborhood, I began to compare it with my own and Marisol's.

El Polvorín, the neighborhood where Ana lived, had pink, yellow, and green houses that looked like flowers on a birthday cake. But they were wood houses with A-shaped tin roofs. Wood houses were often blown down by hurricanes or destroyed by termites. Anybody who could afford it lived in a concrete block house with a flat roof—like I did. Or they lived in a house with curved roof tiles, like Marisol did. So although Ana wasn't as poor as Nora—who lived in San Antón and went to Cordero only because she got a scholarship—Ana still was kind of poor. More or less like Abuelita.

It wasn't as if I hadn't noticed the way Ana lived before. I had. But it had never seemed important.

Don Toño parked his taxi in front of Ana's house, which was light yellow and had no carport. He got out of the car when we did, and came to say goodbye. He was short and skinny—a little bit shorter and skinnier than Doña Monse. He hugged her, then kissed Ana on her forehead. "I love you!"

"I love you too," Ana told him.

Then he pulled on one of my curls. "Have fun, but don't celebrate that marshmallow wedding until tomorrow. Because I want to be in it."

I giggled. "Okay."

After he left, Doña Monse opened the front door of the house, and we hurried in, crossing through a living room that only had rocking chairs—no sofas.

Ana spilled the candies on the dining-room table. "What kind of gifts should we give the bride and groom?" she asked me.

I studied the candies on the plastic tablecloth. "We should give them a marshmallow bed with miniature marshmallow pillows."

Ana smiled. "We can also give them M&M's wrapped in tissue paper. And . . . Hershey's kisses."

I clapped. "Invitations! We have to send invitations or they won't get any gifts."

Ana's nose twitched in a smile. "I thought about that already." She showed me a bag of candy hearts.

"Perfect! Let's send a heart invitation to the Chiclets family and another to . . . these mint twins."

"Well, if you're going to invite them, we should invite the *Pilones*."

*Pilones* were homemade hard candies on a stick. I couldn't see any on the table, so I asked, "Do you have *pilones*?"

"No, but we can go to El Jíbaro and buy some."

On the way to El Jíbaro, we walked by a stray dog that was scrounging trash out of a garbage can. There were lots of stray dogs in Ana's neighborhood. Some of them had bloody, scabby patches on their skin, a disgusting rash called *sarna*.

We also walked by a house where somebody was loudly playing "*Que bonita bandera,* how beautiful the Puerto Rican flag is." I found this cheerful, but Mami would have called it inconsiderate noise.

"Mami wants to send me to La Academia," I told Ana after we'd passed the house.

Ana made a face as if she'd eaten a sour candy. "She does?"

I nodded. "She wants me to be like La Academia girls."

Ana stepped in front of me and, walking backward, asked, "Do you?"

"Well . . . no."

Ana's curly eyelashes blinked. She turned around and stomped the last few steps to El Jíbaro. I'd planned to tell her about Marisol and her Ginny dolls, and her shoes, and her uniforms—all those things we could probably have if we went to La Academia. But Ana seemed so upset that I decided to keep it to myself.

El Jíbaro was just a stand with bananas, pineapples, and mangoes hanging in front, and big glass jars of candy on its counter. That day one of the jars had *ajonjolí*, candies made out of sesame seeds.

"Should we invite the *Ajonjolí* family?" Ana asked.

I pointed at another jar. "And the *Pilones*."

"*¡Caramba!*" the owner of El Jíbaro said when he saw us. "You girls are sure growing!"

"Thank you," Ana said.

"You're not supposed to say thank you when somebody says you've grown," I whispered to her after she'd asked for the candies and the man had turned to find a bag.

"Why?"

"How many people have you heard saying thank you when they're told they're taller?"

Ana shrugged. "Nobody, but that doesn't mean it's wrong."

"I'm not saying it's wrong. But if other people don't do it, we shouldn't either."

I was just trying to teach Ana social manners so she could go to La Academia with me. I also wanted to tell her that she was too old to wear dresses with bows in back, and bobby socks, and shoes with buckles. But before I could do that, I had to stop wearing them myself, and I didn't know how to break the news to Mami.

"What are you going to do with all this candy?" the man in El Jíbaro asked, giving us the *pilones* and *ajonjolí*.

We told him about the marshmallow wedding, and he gave us *marrayos,* grated coconut candies. "Gifts for the bride and groom."

On our way to the house, we ate the *marrayos*.

We were not hungry for dinner, but Doña Monse made us eat leftover rice with pigeon beans. I hated pigeon beans! They looked and tasted like tiny, greenish-brown plastic purses. With the fork I pecked them to the side of the plate and ate the yellow rice.

Waiting for Doña Monse to finish her meal, I said, "The bride can be Marsha Mallow and the groom can be Marshall Mint." American names, I thought, because they would be made out of American candies.

I knew I'd done well because Ana and her mother gave me dimpled smiles. Ana did well too. She called the priest Father Goodbar.

After dinner, we tried different food coloring on the marshmallows. Those we didn't like, we ate. We ended up with a blue suit for the groom, a yellow one for the best man, and pink dresses for the bridesmaids. Then we began to make people out of marshmallows held together with toothpicks.

I made the driver with long, long legs.

"Why did you do that?" Ana asked.

"Wedding cars are long, so the driver's legs have to be long."

"Well, my father is a driver, and he doesn't have long legs."

"But your father is just a taxi driver." I didn't mean to say it that way. It just slipped out of my mouth.

Ana threw a bridesmaid on the table. "Shorten his legs or we won't have a marshmallow wedding."

"Don't be stupid!" That slipped out too.

"You're getting stuck up, you know. First La Academia, and now you're poking fun at my father!"

"No, I'm not!"

"You are! You are!" Ana stomped to her bedroom, crying.

Her mother, who had been washing dishes in the kitchen, followed her.

I stayed in the dining room, making marshmallow people and thinking that I wanted to go home. I wanted to call Mami and tell her to pick me up. I knew she would, but I had to ask permission to use the phone, and I didn't want to.

After a few minutes Doña Monse came out. "Ana ate too many candies. She'll feel better in the morning."

That made me think that Ana hadn't told her everything I'd said.

I began to clean up with Doña Monse's help. I didn't say a word to her. I felt bad about what I'd said to Ana but also angry. I told myself that it wasn't polite to leave guests alone. I bet that in high society they would never call guests names and leave them alone.

After we finished cleaning up, Doña Monse sent me to bed.

I lifted Ana's stupid mosquito net. At home we didn't use mosquito nets. We had window screens. I lay down, my head at the foot of the four-poster bed, by Ana's feet. Usually a cool breeze came in through Ana's window, but the air was thick that night. Some mosquitoes circled my head. I swatted them over to Ana's side. But they came back because Ana had covered herself from head to toe. I tried to do the same, but it was *so* hot. I lay there sweating, and finally fell asleep thinking about being an Academia girl.

# 6

*Barrunto.* That was what Mami called the hot, stuffy air before it rains.

The *barrunto* and all those mixed-up feelings about Ana, La Academia, and me kept me hot all night at Ana's house.

The *barrunto* did bring rain, and it woke me up with its pianolike music on the tin roof. A breeze danced through the mosquito net and, on and off, the soft net touched my face and leg. I lay still, thinking about what had happened the night before. I hadn't meant to poke fun at Ana's father. I liked him. I'd told Ana that many times.

Maybe I shouldn't have told Ana about La Academia. That was probably the real reason she'd been upset. I was upset because of La Academia too. I felt wobbly. One moment I didn't want to leave Cordero. The next moment I wanted to try La Academia and have all those pretty things Marisol had. But I didn't want to leave Ana and Miss Bocachica behind—if only they could come with me.

The tin-roof music didn't sound like a piano anymore. It was louder. The sound, now like calypso tin drums, woke up Ana. I stared at her. "Are you still mad at me?"

She rubbed her eyes and shook her head.

"I'll shorten the driver's legs, okay?" I said.

Ana just waved—enough for me to know that everything was okay between us. Ana had a quick temper, but she also was quick to forgive.

A man's voice on her parents' bedroom radio announced the time—a quarter to seven—and Ana jumped out of bed. She took a mantilla out of her dresser.

"Hurry up, Tere." She peered at me in the mirror, coils of hair dangling across her face. "I don't want to be late for church, because if we are, my father will make us stay for another Mass, and we won't have enough time for the marshmallow wedding."

I'd forgotten that Ana and her parents went to church at eight. My parents and I went to the ten o'clock Mass. I preferred the earlier time because Sundays seemed longer, with more time to play.

We got dressed in each other's clothes—Ana in a pique dress Mami had made me; I wore a red-and-yellow outfit with many ruffles that Ana had bought at Felipe García. But today it didn't look as pretty, because it wasn't an outfit an Academia girl would wear. I felt like telling Ana that I wanted to wear my own dress, but I didn't want to hurt her feelings again.

We had to fast for at least three hours before receiving Communion, so we left without breakfast. It was raining so hard that Don Toño drove us into the plaza itself, all the way to the cathedral entrance. He left us there and went to park his taxi.

Inside the church, we put on our mantillas and made the sign of the cross with the holy water in the shell-shaped basin. Then Don Toño came in. He put his dripping umbrella by the church door and we followed him and Doña Monse through the middle aisle to a pew close to a confessional box. We knelt on the kneeling bench. Ana put her hands together, closed her eyes, and prayed. I prayed a quick Our Father and sat.

A line of people stood at each side of the confessional box. One of the priests—probably Padre Mario—was sitting in the little room in the middle. A purple curtain covered most of his body, but his black cassock and his feet leaned toward the side, where a girl with white patent-leather shoes was confessing. I wondered if that girl had real sins to confess.

Whenever I went to confession and told Padre Mario one of my sins, he'd ask me, "What else?" I'd tell him another sin and he'd ask again, "What else?" Sometimes I didn't have any more sins, but I felt I had to tell him another. One day I made a list of sins to tell him. First on the list were my real sins, like "I haven't always been good to my friends and parents." I made up others, like "I've said many bad words, I haven't been nice to my teacher, I've stolen a candy and eaten it." I told them all to Padre Mario, then said, "I lied." This last one was really true because I lied to the priest about all those sins I'd made up.

The priest came out of the sacristy followed by two altar boys. That meant that the Mass had started.

~~~~

I stood up with everybody else, and my mantilla fell from my head to my shoulder. Ana fixed it for me, mostly because she wanted my attention. She liked to goof off in church. I did, too, but the Sunday before, I'd started a game in church, and I wanted to try it again.

Miss Bocachica had always said it was okay to read slowly as long as we understood what we were reading and as long as we enjoyed it. But I wanted to begin reading my missal when the Mass started and try to finish reading it by the time the Mass ended.

I began on time and read and read, even when Ana elbowed me, even while the priest gave the sermon, even when I went to take Communion. But *caramba,* when the Mass ended, I was reading the Offertory, halfway into my missal.

❧

It hardly rained in Ponce, but when it rained, it poured! On the way to Ana's house a curtain of rain covered the windshield, and Don Toño leaned forward, trying to see through. I read again and again the sign on the dashboard: *DIOS ILUMINE NUESTRO CAMINO* because I thought we could have an accident. But Don Toño took us safely to the house.

After we changed clothes and ate breakfast, Ana and I finished the last details of the marshmallow wedding—which for me included shortening the driver's legs.

Don Toño played the wedding march on his guitar. Ana pretended to be Marsha Mallow, the bride. I did Marshall Mint, Father Goodbar, and the driver. Doña

Monse was the bride's mother, who cried and cried. And Ana and I took turns with the bridesmaids.

At the reception Don Toño played a waltz, and Ana and I danced. She was holding the bride. I held the groom. Don Toño rested his guitar against a wall and, humming the waltz, cut in. Ana danced with her father, and I danced with her mother.

We also opened the candy gifts and ate them. We cut the wedding cupcake in half and ate it. When the time came for the bride and groom to leave, we took them on a honeymoon trip—right into our mouths. As each guest said good-bye, we ate them too.

When we were sent to bed that evening, I went reluctantly. It had been a fun day, and I didn't want it to end. In bed I talked to Ana about all the fun I'd always had with her.

"Me too," she said.

After that, she answered, *"Ajá, ajá, a . . . "* Then no answer. She was sound asleep.

It took me awhile, but I finally fell asleep, too, listening to the rain that was still playing music on the tin roof.

# 7

*T*iny birds called *reinitas* woke us, announcing with their songs that it had stopped raining. While Ana stretched, I knelt on the bed and looked outside. The *reinitas* flew down to the stairs where Doña Monse had placed plates of rice and water. They drank, but they really didn't need water. The rain had flooded the street drains, and the neighborhood dogs drank water from the curbs. The *reinitas* could have done the same, but I guessed they were from a better class than the mangy dogs.

After a cornflakes breakfast, Don Toño took us to school. We sat in the backseat of the taxi. Usually, if Doña Monse wasn't coming, Ana sat in front with her father. Mami didn't think it was proper for a woman or girl to sit in front with a taxi driver. Ana could because the driver was her father. I couldn't.

Some Academia girls went to school in taxis, and I felt important. But nobody I knew saw us on the way to school.

The arch of purple and orange *trinitaria* flowers sprinkled us with raindrops as we walked through the school gate. I dumped my book bag by the classroom and went back to Ana, who had stayed by the hedge, sipping hibiscus nectar like a hummingbird. I plucked off a hibiscus, turned it upside down, and sucked up all its juice.

Humming the "Blue Danube" waltz, I spun the hibiscus, using the top of the hedge as a stage. Ana's flower joined mine. We twirled the flowers, bringing them together, then apart, raindrops sprinkling out like sparkling sequins falling from skirts.

Wiping off a drop that fell on my cheek, I saw Linda coming. She ran toward us and tagged me. "You're . . . " She stared at our flowers. "Those look like carnival gowns!"

"They are!" Ana spun her flower again and asked Linda, "Are you going to enter the Cordero carnival contest?"

"Yes! Are you?"

Ana nodded, and I said, "*Ajá,* I can hardly wait."

"I can't either." Linda closed her eyes and spun around and around, her hands to her side as if she were wearing a gown.

In third grade Miss Bocachica had given Linda's mother money to help pay for Linda's outfit for a school play. So I knew Linda's family couldn't afford a gown. We probably couldn't either. Still, it was exciting to talk about the carnival and our gowns.

Linda stopped spinning and opened her eyes, blinking—waking up from her dream.

"Let's play tag," she finally said, tagging me again. "*Te quedas,* you're It!"

I dropped my flower, reached for Ana's hand,

tagged her, and ran! I glanced back. Ana dumped her book bag by the classroom and ran toward me. "She's coming!" I yelled.

Linda and I fled in different directions.

A few days ago the ground had been a cracked linoleum of dry mud. Now it was a squishy carpet of soft mud and rotten leaves. Mud splattered my legs, but I didn't care. I just didn't want to be tagged. I ran and ran, zigzagging, trying not to hit other children. I jumped over puddles and held on to the swing set that had no swings.

Ana ran toward Cesar, who had his brown hands cupped under the faucet to drink water.

"Ana is It," Linda yelled to him.

He tried to run, but before he could finish turning off the faucet, Ana had tagged him. I bounced happily because I didn't really want Ana to be It. I'd tagged her because I didn't want to be It either.

I went, "Nyah-nyah, nyah-nyah-nyah-nyah," to Cesar. He chased me through the swing set and around the *níspero* tree. He almost tagged me, but missed when Ana and Linda distracted him, saying, "Nyah-nyah, nyah-nyah-nyah-nyah." He ran after them.

After the two-day sleep-over at Ana's, I felt tired. I walked to a puddle and waited for my friends, poking holes in the mud with the toe of my loafer.

I heard Linda. "Nyah-nyah-nyah-nyah."

I looked up.

"*Te quedas,*" Cesar said. "You're It!"

*¡Pángana!* Paf! He hit my back, and I sprawled facedown in the mud puddle.

At first Cesar laughed, but then he said, "Here, let me help you."

Too angry to give him my hand, I clawed the mud, trying to get up by myself. But my knee caught on the hem of my skirt, tearing it and making me fall again.

Cesar held my hand, and this time I let him pull me up, my body sounding like a rubber mat on a bathtub. When I made it all the way up, Linda laughed. It wasn't funny. My eyes were blurred by the stinging mix of mud—and tears that wouldn't stop.

"My shoe!" I cried. I had one loafer on, but not the other.

I dug in the mud blindly with my feet but couldn't feel the shoe.

Nora found it and handed it to me.

The bell rang and I stood there like a bronze statue with a shoe in my hand.

"Let's clean you up," Ana said, walking me to the faucet.

"What happened?" other children asked.

"She fell in the mud," Linda answered.

The bell rang, but nobody lined up. They stayed around the faucet, watching Ana and Cesar filling their cupped hands with water and pouring it over my uniform.

"What's going on?" Miss Bocachica asked, breaking the circle. She gasped. "What happened?"

"It's my fault," Cesar said.

Miss Bocachica shook her head. "Ana, please, walk Teresa home."

Cesar patted my back. "I'm sorry."

I didn't answer.

On the way home Ana and I didn't talk. I felt yucky. My shirt clung to my chest, and the torn hem flapped against my knee, dripping mud.

Ana rang our doorbell.

When Mami opened the door and gasped, Ana almost choked in an outburst of words. "We were playing tag and Cesar accidentally tagged Tere a little bit too hard and she fell facedown in the mud and Miss Bocachica asked me to bring her home."

"Thank you, Ana." Mami took my bag from her. "You can go back to school."

Mami closed the door, dropped my bag on the floor, and rushed me to the bathroom. "You see, Teresa? Cordero isn't a school for a sweet girl like you. You should go to La Academia de Niñas, where you won't have to deal with rough boys like Cesar."

"Mami, Cesar isn't . . . rough . . ."

My voice cracked like dry mud.

*I* felt bad about my fall, mostly because Mami kept mentioning it. But at school nobody talked about it. We just got really busy planning Miss Bocachica's wedding shower party.

Principal Galí knew all about it. The day of the party he called Miss Bocachica to his office so we could decorate her desk with flowers that Linda had made out of Kleenex. We also decorated my umbrella with the same kind of flowers and taped it to Miss Bocachica's chair. Then Ana went to tell her that she had to come right away because we had gone wild.

When she came in, we cried, "Surprise!"

She was surprised, but she was more so when she saw the gifts. "You shouldn't have done this." Her eyes were teary.

She opened each gift carefully, though we were all on top of her saying, "Open mine! Open mine!"

Linda gave her a clay vase; Cesar, pillowcases; Luis, a picture frame; Nora, pot holders. Miss Bocachica liked them all, but I didn't think she could possibly like mine as much as Ana's glass swan. I'd asked Mami to buy a silver platter for Miss Bocachica, but Mami sewed place mats instead.

After the gifts were opened, Miguel put the blender he'd brought from his house on his desk. Then he plugged it in. I poured in the milk to make a milkshake called *champola*. Miss Bocachica opened a can of guava chunks for us, and I dumped in the whole thing, filling up the container. Miguel pressed the MIX button.

"Put the lid on!" Miss Bocachica yelled.

Too late. The pink *champola* and its guava chunks arched out. Miguel put the lid on. The *champola* kept spilling out. I tried to press the OFF button but, under the downpour of *champola*, I pushed the wrong button. It made the whole thing go faster! More *champola* poured out.

Finally, I pushed the right button. The blender stopped and the *champola* settled down.

Cesar clapped. "That was fun!"

Miss Bocachica shook her head, smiling. It surprised me that she could smile. The *champola* was still dripping on Miguel's desk and onto the floor. I wiped off his desk with the party napkins, but they quickly turned into a mushy pulp.

Luis, Nora, and Linda, who had made a circle to see what was happening, jumped on the *champola* pool, splattering the sticky mess.

"Don't!" Ana told them.

"Sit down, please." Miss Bocachica directed us to our desks.

She covered the pool on the floor with old towels, then served and gave us half-full paper cups of *cham-*

*pola*. It was good! Soon my cup was empty. I wished most of the *champola* hadn't spilled.

Miss Bocachica sat on her chair, still in the middle of the room with my umbrella attached to it. She drank all of her *champola*. After placing her cup on the floor, she reached for a long piece of chalk. "Children, I have an announcement to make."

She'd used the same words when she announced her engagement. This time, though, her voice sounded different. She broke the chalk in half, took each half, and broke it. "After the wedding," she finally said, "I won't be coming back to school."

"Why?" I cried, remembering that Mami had said that Miss Bocachica probably would move.

"Tsk!" Ana said in a smart way. "Because she's taking some days off for the honeymoon."

"Is that it?" I asked.

Miss Bocachica stared down at her ring and tapped the diamond with a piece of chalk. "No, I'm not coming back to Cordero School. Not even after the honeymoon."

"Why?" My voice came out bubbly, the way it did when I talked with my head under the shower.

"I learned last night"—Miss Bocachica turned to put the pieces of chalk on the blackboard railing—"that the army is moving my fiancé to a fort in Oklahoma. I'll have to move with him."

Mami was right. Miss Bocachica was leaving. *¡Ay!*

"Oklahoma? That far?" That was Cesar, who knew the United States because he'd lived in New York.

"That far" for me meant that we might not see her again. I didn't want to think about it. With my bottom teeth I unrolled the ring on the rim of the paper cup, collecting the wax as I went around it. I unstuck the wax from the back of my teeth and swallowed it. I coughed. A tear rolled out. Without Miss Bocachica, I didn't want to stay in Rafael Cordero School.

"Who's going to be our teacher?" Linda asked.

"Mrs. Ortega."

"She's mean." Linda again. "She hits children with rulers."

"No, she doesn't," Miss Bocachica said.

"She does," Linda insisted. "The eighth graders had her as a substitute, and they told me."

"They said that to scare you. But she doesn't."

The bell rang, and some of the children sprang out of their seats as if this was any ordinary day. I watched them pack their book bags, but I stayed sitting down.

"Don't forget that today is my last day," Miss Bocachica said. "Whenever you're ready, come and give me a hug."

Nora got ready first. Miss Bocachica hugged her and said something into her ear. It must have been good because Nora left the room smiling. Others lined up to hug her. Linda gave her a long hug. Cesar did too.

I turned to look at Ana. Like me, she'd stayed in her seat. Her *níspero*-seed eyes, almond shaped and shiny, were full of tears.

I squeezed my paper cup and stared at the ceiling fan. The breeze kept my eyes dry, but my throat hurt. Like a kinked hose full of water, I was about to burst. Slowly, I lowered my head and let the tears rush out.

Miss Bocachica had stretched out her arms. "My girls, it's time to go home."

With nobody else in the room, Ana and I felt okay to bury our faces in our teacher's shoulders and cry on her blue blouse. Her warm brown arms stayed around us for a long time.

"We need tissue," Miss Bocachica said, and stood up to get a box.

"Why are we crying?" she asked, after drying her tears. She threw her tissue in the waste basket, took another, and began to dry my tears. "You're both coming to my wedding, aren't you?"

Ana and I nodded. Miss Bocachica patted dry a tear that rolled down Ana's neck. "Let's think about that happy day. Okay? Now, run home. Your mothers are waiting for you."

Without saying a word to each other, Ana and I walked out and went to sit in the shade of the *níspero* tree. I picked up a *níspero* and peeled part of its skin. I took a bite but threw the rest against the fence. "I can't believe it."

"I can't either. How can she leave us?"

"After so many years with her, how can we get used to anyone else?" I cleared my throat because my voice had come out bubbly again.

Ana snapped a *níspero* branch and tapped her forefinger on the milky gum seeping out. She rolled the gluey stuff between her thumb and forefinger.

"I don't want to be here if Miss Bocachica isn't." I hit the ground with the heel of my loafer. "We should change schools. We should go to La Academia de Niñas."

Ana faced me. Her eyes were swollen from all the crying, but she had them wide open. "Tere, my parents can't afford La Academia."

"But La Academia has scholarships!" I said.

"Yes, Tere," Ana said. "But I don't want to go to La Academia. And I don't want you to go either. Look, Miss Bocachica is leaving, but I have you and you have me."

"That's true." I pulled gently on one of her braids and smiled. "Okay, we'll stay here."

**9**

On the night of Miss Bocachica's wedding, the glass on the church chandeliers sparkled like raindrops when the sun comes out. A white carpet ran down the center aisle, and the pews were decorated with white and pink bows.

"The girls can sit in the front pew, don't you think?" Doña Monse asked Mami.

"I don't see why not. It's not reserved. But girls," Mami added, frowning at Ana, "no talking and no giggling during the ceremony. Understand?"

Ana and I nodded, and walked toward the altar hand in hand. As I entered the pew, my golden-brown dress made the *rik-rik* noise tulle makes. Ana touched the layers of tulle and the bouquet of velvet forget-me-nots on my shoulder.

"You look so pretty!"

I felt really good about my dress, but I didn't know what to say. I could tell Ana that she looked pretty too, but she knew better. She was wearing her green cotton Christmas dress, now too small for her.

"Thanks," I finally said. "This is the dress Mami made."

We sat by the center aisle, where we could see the bride coming. I spread my skirt on the pew. Then

I saw Ana sitting too far away, and I gathered my skirt in. "Move closer," I said, and she moved until our arms touched.

A woman sitting in the pew across from us turned, and glanced toward the entrance. "That's Miss Bocachica's mother," Ana whispered.

The woman's dark, wrinkled face didn't look like Miss Bocachica's, but Ana had to be right, because the woman was wearing a corsage.

A man dressed in an army uniform, followed by Padre Mario, came out of the sacristy and stood between two baskets of pink carnations. I'd never seen anybody with skin so dark in my life! He carried his army hat under his arm. The hair at the sides of his head had been shaved off, but a square had been left on top. The clump of hair coiled like black wire.

Ana whispered, "That must be the man Miss Bocachica is marrying."

"He's black!"

"So what? Miss Bocachica is black too."

"She *is*?"

"Come on, Tere. Miss Bocachica has been your teacher since first grade and you didn't know she was black? What color did you think she was?"

I shrugged. "Brown."

Ana's eyes met mine. "What color do you think I am?"

"Brown."

Ana shook her head. "I'm black too."

I couldn't believe it! To me, for somebody to be

black, she or he had to be really black and have full lips and a wide nose like Nora's or like the groom's. Ana and Miss Bocachica were not like that.

"You're not black," I insisted.

"I am. Look at my parents." Before I could turn around, she added, "And at my hair."

"I have curly hair too."

"But you have good hair. Mine is *pelo malo,* bad, nappy."

I wanted to shout: "You don't have bad hair! And I know what brown is; you're *níspero* brown!" But what did I know? Maybe that shade of brown was called black when it was a skin color.

The wedding march began, and we stood up. My eyes moved slowly toward the back of the church as I studied each guest along the pews across from us. So many different shades of brown skin! It was as if they had been black coffee and somebody—probably God—had come along to pour milk in them. Some had so much milk, they looked white; some had less milk; others less yet; others none. Which ones were called black? How much milk did they need to be called white?

This wedding wasn't like our marshmallow one. No bridesmaid walked down the aisle, just Miss Bocachica and her father. She was beautiful! Appliqué decorated with pearls and clear sequins covered the center of her white satin gown and its puffy sleeves. The sequins sparkled as much as the church chandeliers.

I wished Miss Bocachica would notice me, but she passed by us, staring straight ahead—straight at the groom. She kissed her father, his bald head shiny brown like my teacher's skin—which still looked brown to me, not black. The groom took Miss Bocachica by the elbow and walked her to the altar.

Everybody sat down. Ana's arm touched mine, and I compared them. Ana *was* browner than me, but I wasn't as white as Linda or Marisol. And when I went to Las Cucharas Beach, I got darker yet. I didn't have nappy hair, but it was curly. Maybe I was black too.

I looked back. Ana's parents were *tintos,* coffee without milk. Mami, who was wearing a beautiful royal-blue chiffon dress, was milky white. And Papi? He looked like *café con leche,* coffee with a lot of milk.

Mami twirled her finger, telling me to turn around and pay attention to the ceremony. I did. The train of Miss Bocachica's gown went all the way down the altar steps. I decided to have a long train like hers in my wedding. But I wanted little children to carry it when I entered the church. And I wanted a flower girl in front of me, throwing flowers in my path. And my bridesmaids would be girls my age now, between nine and ten. And Ana would be my maid of honor!

Miss Bocachica and the groom exchanged rings and said to each other, "I do." Then Padre Mario gave them his blessing. When the groom kissed Miss Bocachica on her lips, Ana poked me with her elbow. We giggled.

After the photographer took many pictures, the

wedding march began again. On the way down the aisle Miss Bocachica pointed at us and said something to her husband. He winked at us. I liked his wink.

Everybody went out and rushed to their cars to follow the bride and groom's convertible to the reception at Miss Bocachica's house.

"We'll see you there." Doña Monse waved.

"Can I go with them?" I asked.

"No," Mami said. "This is a family outing, and you should at least ride with us."

Reluctantly, I went with them.

Papi followed the parade of cars, everybody else honking their car horns. "Papi, honk!" I said. "Honk!"

Mami placed her hand on Papi's hand and honked, her hand so much lighter than Papi's! I studied my hand. "What color am I?"

They stopped honking. Papi glanced at Mami. "What did she say?" he asked.

I leaned forward from the backseat, my head between them. "I want to know what color I am."

"That's what I thought you said."

"White, of course." I heard Mami say over the outside honking.

"But I'm not as white as Linda or Marisol."

"That's because you're olive white," Mami said.

"What kind of olive? Green or black?"

Papi hit the steering wheel and burst out laughing. "The olive color comes from your mother's family."

"No, it doesn't." Mami hit Papi's arm playfully. "Your French ancestors were the ones who mixed themselves with everybody."

*"Y tu abuela, ¿dónde está?"* Papi recited. "And your grandma, where is she?"

I'd heard the poem before. It said that everybody has the blood of a black grandma.

"I didn't have black grandmas," Mami cried. "Look at Abuelita! She's whiter than white. She has pure Spanish blood, and so did my father."

"Are you sure that back in Spain somebody in your family didn't mix with the Moors?"

"I told you. We're pure white."

"You don't like black people, do you?"

"It's not that, Ramón."

"Come on, would you have married me if I were black?"

I expected Mami to say "Sure," but she shook her head no.

That hit my stomach like a concrete block.

"I can't help it, Ramón. These are feelings I was born with."

"No, Dolores, nobody is born with those feelings. We learn them, and they can be unlearned."

*"Ajá,* just as easy as you have unlearned yours. Anyway, Ramón," Mami said between teeth, "this isn't a good time to discuss this."

She turned her head and stared out the passenger window. But Papi drew her toward him and touched her head with his head. "I do love you, Dolores. It's just that . . ."

"I love you, too, Ramón. But sometimes you get on my nerves."

Mami did love Papi—she really had to dislike

blacks to say that she wouldn't marry him if he were black.

Now I knew why she didn't want me to marry any-body from Cordero. It was because they were black. *Ajá*. Cesar was a doctor's son, but he and his father were darker than Ana. They were black—not brown, as I'd thought. Luis was black too. I'd known about Nora, but not about them. But Mami knew.

And Ana could *never* be of high society, because she was black.

I shook my head. I'd always loved Ana—and Miss Bocachica and even Cesar—and I wasn't going to stop loving them because now I knew they were black.

~

Ana was waiting for me in front of the carport of Miss Bocachica's modern, concrete block house.

"Wait until you see the wedding cake," Ana said as soon as I got to her.

"You saw the cake already?"

"*Ajá*," she said, walking in. "We were the first ones here, and I got to hug Miss Bocachica before any-body else."

I wanted to hug Miss Bocachica too, but she and her husband were standing under a white arch, and a long line of people waited to congratulate them. So I went with Ana to see the cake.

We ran around the table and peeked under the frosting-covered bridges. Under each bridge swam two white plastic swans. The pond where they swam was just a round mirror. But the wedding cake itself had on its very top a fountain shooting out real water.

"I wonder how the fountain works." Ana lifted the white tablecloth and disappeared under the table.

I looked around to see if anybody had seen her, then Miss Bocachica saw me. "My wonderful girl, come and give me a hug." She kneeled, and her wedding gown belled out. We hugged. A line of little buttons went down her back. I wanted a dress with buttons like that.

Then Miss Bocachica's husband offered me his hand. I put my hand on his pink palm. He held my fingers gently. "I've heard good things about you."

I let go, and skipped to tell Ana that I'd shook hands with the groom. "He's really nice," she said. "Let's go see the gifts."

A blender, a nightgown, two irons, a set of glasses, and many other gifts were displayed on Miss Bocachica's bed. But on her pillow she had the gifts the Cordero children had given her, a Kleenex flower by each of them.

"Neat!" we said, glancing at each other.

Then we heard the accordion playing the waltz, and we ran to the carport to see the bride and groom dancing, looking at each other. *So* romantic. Many of the grown-ups cut in to dance with them. Then Miss Bocachica and her husband danced together again.

Ana and I had been too shy to cut in and dance with the groom or even with the bride. But after the waltz, the accordion player began to play a *pasodoble,* and Miss Bocachica asked Ana to dance. Her husband asked me. He pretended he had castanets, and snapped his fingers, dancing around me. Then he took my hands and spun me until my feet lifted off the floor. I probably looked like a flying swing from *La silla voladora,* my most favorite ride at our patron saint's fair. After a while, he slowed down and, little by little, lowered me. I was dizzy. And I loved it!

We switched. Miss Bocachica danced with me, Ana with him. I twirled around Miss Bocachica's fingers like a ballerina doll in a jewelry box. When the song ended, we hugged for a long time.

Then Miss Bocachica's husband came in with a basket full of *capias,* party souvenirs. Miss Bocachica took a *capia* and pinned it on my shoulder. The round piece of gathered white tulle held two tiny golden wedding rings in the center. Two pink ribbons hung at the bottom. One read "Isabel y Carlos"; the other had the wedding date: *7 de octubre de 1961.* Miss Bocachica turned to pin a *capia* on Ana's dress, and I skipped away to show mine to my parents, who were dancing a slow *bolero.*

"It's nice, Teresa," Mami said, then she whispered to Papi, "People don't give *capias* at parties anymore."

Papi frowned. Mami was putting down Miss Bocachica's wedding, and that hurt. I sat in the back-yard and played with the plastic swans decorating a table, crashing them against each other again and again. Why did Mami have to ruin it all? Why did she have to put down everything I loved?

"Come, Tere, let's dance."

I stood up and followed Ana, thinking that I could not possibly have fun. But I did.

Ana and I danced more *pasodobles* and *merengues* and *plenas*. We danced many times with the bride, with the groom, with our parents, and with each other. We also spun to the rhythm of the music, making our dresses look like open umbrellas.

Neither of us caught the bouquet. But after Miss Bocachica and her husband cut the cake, we got to eat many pink frosting flowers.

Then I saw Miss Bocachica wearing a blue dress. The time had come for her to leave.

"Here's some rice to throw at the bride and groom." Ana gave me a small tulle sack tied with a ribbon.

I began to follow Ana to the front yard, but I stopped when I saw Miss Bocachica's mother sitting in the backyard alone. Tears flowed down her raisin-like cheeks. I wanted to go to her and tell her that I also was sad, that I didn't want Miss Bocachica to leave, that I'd miss my dear teacher a whole bunch. But I was too shy. I just stood there for a long time— too long. When I finally got to the front yard, Miss Bocachica was gone. Too late to throw the rice and wish her good luck.

A week after Miss Bocachica's wedding Mami and I went to Marisol's house. Marisol tried on the lilac dress Mami had made.

"Pretty!" Marisol cried, looking at herself in the mirror.

"I love it too," Doña Carlota said. "You can wear it for your birthday party."

My first thought was: Would I be invited to Marisol's birthday?

Then Mami sighed, and grinned, and I got it! This meant they had hired her to make Marisol's carnival gown. And maybe I could go to La Academia. Then for sure I'd be invited to Marisol's birthday party!

Yet I knew that the payment from one gown couldn't pay the tuition. Besides, I'd told Ana that I'd stay at Cordero School.

Marisol changed clothes, then signaled me to follow her. Outside the family room she whispered, "My mother sprinkled a white powder on the living room floor, and it's a lot of fun to skate in there."

"I thought you were not supposed to play in the living room."

"We are not. But we're going to."

She opened the spooky living room door and

began to skate in the white powder as if she had ice-skated every day of her life. "Come!"

I shook my head, looking toward the family room where Mami and Doña Carlota were.

"Don't be silly. It's fun!"

She held my hands and pulled me in. We skated together and, when I'd gotten the hang of it, she let go. My legs turned into Jell-O, and I wobbled all over the place. *¡Kataplum!* I fell.

I laughed. "This stuff is like soap!"

I tried to get up. *¡Kataplum!* I fell again.

"Let me help you," Marisol said, laughing too.

She tried to get me up, but *¡kataplum-plum-plum!* We both fell.

"What are you doing?" I heard Doña Carlota say.

We glanced at each other and quickly crawled out of the living room. We ran to the backyard before our mothers could catch us. Outside, we laughed and laughed. Our clothes were covered with white powder. We tried to wipe it off, but it stayed on. So Marisol pulled me to the garden sprinkler and we took a shower.

"Ah!" Doña Carlota said when she came out with Mami. "They're just playing."

Mami sighed. "It looks as if they are going to be good friends."

"*Ajá.*" Doña Carlota nodded. "They have only been together a couple of times, but they seem to like each other. I'm pleased because Teresa is such a nice girl and because I want Marisol to have friends outside La Academia's circle."

I was glad that Doña Carlota wanted me to be Marisol's friend—and relieved that we had gotten away with what we'd done.

Unfortunately I didn't get out of the next one.

⌒

The following afternoon I was sitting at my desk, thinking about the skating while Mrs. Ortega erased the arithmetic problems we'd just finished working on. There were big differences between Mrs. Ortega and Miss Bocachica.

Mrs. Ortega had dark hair and dark skin, yet her eyes were as clear as blue marbles. They could have been pretty eyes, but because the eighth graders had said that Mrs. Ortega hit children, I thought she had vampire eyes.

Also, unlike Miss Bocachica, Mrs. Ortega didn't believe we knew as much as we did. When she read anything in English, she repeated it in Spanish as if we didn't understand English. And she had a difficult time accepting that girls could be good in arithmetic. Every time any of us did a problem correctly, she asked if the boys had helped us.

Nobody liked her. She wasn't Miss Bocachica.

"I have to get something from the office," she said after she finished erasing the board. "I'll be back in a minute."

It wasn't going to be a minute. The few days she'd been our teacher, she'd left us alone a lot—for long periods, as if she really didn't want to be with us.

As soon as she left, I said, "Who dares make soap *champola* and skate on it?"

I kind of meant it as a joke. But Nora was the only one who said, "Are you kidding? We would get in trouble if we do that." Everybody else liked the idea.

Everything happened very quickly. Miguel moved his desk to the wall and plugged in the blender, the same blender we'd used at Miss Bocachica's shower, the blender he'd forgotten to take home. Cesar took its container outside and poured water in it. Back inside, he dumped in the tiny bit of soap he'd found by the outside faucet. Then he ran to the boys' bathroom to look for more soap. Meanwhile Ana poured in the milk she didn't drink at lunch.

Worried that we could get caught, I ran to the door to check for Mrs. Ortega.

"Is she coming?" Ana asked.

I peeked out once more. "No, keep going!" I said, thinking that we couldn't get into much trouble if we made the soap *champola* and left it in the blender.

Cesar came back from the bathroom with a thin bar of soap. "This is all I could find."

"I'll go and see if I can find some in the girls' bathroom," I said.

I heard Ana saying, "No, stay where you are and watch for Mrs. Ortega." But Mrs. Ortega wasn't anywhere in sight. I ran to the bathroom, then the end-of-the-day bell rang, and I ran back to the classroom.

I found Mrs. Ortega by the door, watching! Miguel was pouring the soap *champola* on the floor, and everybody else was skating to their desks—sliding, holding on, laughing, shouting.

Mrs. Ortega's vampire eyes peered at me. "What's going on?"

I shrugged, and she screamed, *"Enough!"*

I jumped! Cesar slipped and fell. Linda sputtered and giggled, unable to stop. I also felt like giggling—a nervous giggle—but I bit my tongue. I had to bite it even harder when Mrs. Ortega went slipping and sliding across the room, holding on to desks to keep from falling.

From her desk drawer, she took out a ruler. "Whose idea was this?" she asked, advancing on me.

I didn't want to be hit!

I threw my hands up. "I didn't do anything!" All eyes turned from Mrs. Ortega to me. "I was in the bathroom."

"You said you were going to get soap," Ana whispered, probably thinking I'd forgotten.

Mrs. Ortega lifted the ruler. I panicked! "No, I didn't say that," I lied.

I threw my books in my bag, avoiding Mrs. Ortega's eyes and Ana's.

"Teresa!" Mrs. Ortega tapped the ruler on my desk. "Sit down!"

"She's . . . lying," Ana said. "All this was her idea."

I peered at Ana, not believing what I'd heard! She had tattled on me.

"You're the liar!" I cried. I wished I hadn't said that, but I didn't know how to take it back. So I ran out.

"Teresa!" Mrs. Ortega called. "Teresa, come back here!"

~~~~

She tapped the ruler again. "Nobody leaves this room until it's all clean. Teresa!"

As I ran home, something exploded in me and, all of the sudden, I hated Ana. I thought that Mami was right. Ana could never be in high society. I was better than she was. Much better!

⌐⌐

The kitchen screen door slammed behind me, and Papi, who was washing his hands, glanced at me. Mami stopped peeling a plantain.

"I want to go to La Academia de Niñas," I said, breathless and knowing very well it was the wrong thing to say. But I was angry at Ana, and now everyone at Cordero hated me.

Papi gave Mami a stern look.

Mami threw her hands up, the plantain in one hand, the knife in the other. "Don't look at me like that, Ramón. You were the one who told Teresa to think about which school she wanted to go to. I guess she has finally decided."

"What happened in school today, Teresa?"

"Nothing, Papi. I just want to try La Academia."

Mami winked at me and continued peeling the plantain.

Papi began to dry his hands with a kitchen towel. "I know you miss Miss Bocachica, but you'll get used to it."

"No, I won't." I felt relieved that Papi thought that was why I wanted to switch schools.

"Teresa," he said. "Ana's parents can't afford to send her to La Academia."

"I know she can't go."

"You don't care if you leave her behind?"

"I care," I said, "but I still want to try La Academia."

"Well, I'm not thrilled by the idea, but ladies. . . ." He bowed. "Do whatever you want." He left for his shop without kissing us.

Mami dumped the sliced plantain in salty water. "Teresa, are you sure?"

"Yes, Mami," I said, although I wasn't sure.

"Okay. I'm going to call La Academia."

I didn't think she'd do it, but she did.

Listening to her talk on the phone, I learned that La Academia had a spot for me, and they'd give me the half scholarship, but they needed to see my school records, and I had to pass a test. I didn't want to take a test. If I didn't pass it, I'd have to go back to Cordero and admit I'd lied.

Mami hung up and the phone rang. Mami answered it.

"I'm glad you're calling, because I was about to call you." Mami covered the phone with her hand and whispered to me, "It's Mrs. Ortega."

Mrs. Ortega! I felt like running . . . but, if I did, I'd be in double trouble.

"Did she really?" Mami peered at me and frowned. "No, don't worry about it. I'll talk to her. It won't happen again because we're changing her to La Academia de Niñas. . . . No, no, no, it doesn't have anything to do with what happened today. We just feel she'd fit in better at La Academia. Could you please transfer her records today?" Mami moved her head from side to side as if tired of the conversation. "Yes, I'm sure Teresa will miss Cordero too. . . . No, we made our decision already. . . . Thank you. Thank you."

Mami hung up and sighed. "Teresa, why did you run out of school?"

"Mami, because . . . because Cesar and the others were making soap *champola* in Miguel's blender and, if I'd stayed there, I'd be blamed for the mess."

I couldn't believe myself. Every time I opened my mouth, a lie came out. I worried that Mrs. Ortega had told Mami that the *champola* was my idea and that Mami would catch me lying. But she shook her head. "Cesar, Cesar. *Caramba,* Teresa, am I glad you're going to La Academia."

I felt relieved and, at the same time, sick at heart. I really didn't want to tell how I'd lied. But I wanted to take it all back and have it all be okay again and stay at Cordero.

11

*T*he next morning—way before the school day began—Mami and I walked into the dark hallway of La Academia. It looked dark not only because we'd come from the already bright sun, but also because all the rooms were closed.

Mami asked a woman mopping the floor where the office was, and she showed us. On the way I saw two water coolers, side by side, one taller than the other. I thought it would be nice not to have to drink water from a faucet on the side of the building, like I'd done for years at Cordero.

Before knocking on the office door, Mami held my hand. Freezing. She was at least as nervous as I was.

A lady wearing a necklace with two rows of pearls opened the door, and a splash of cold air-conditioned air hit my face. "You must be Teresa. I am Mrs. Fernández, the principal." She said this peering at me, but shaking hands with Mami.

We sat by her desk. While she asked Mami whether or not I'd had my shots, I studied her red hair. I could tell she dyed it because her eyebrows were as black as tar.

She spread five pictures on her desk. As soon as I saw the spindle and the princess, I knew these were pictures of *Sleeping Beauty*.

"How would you arrange these?"

I'd done an exercise like that in first grade, but it seemed stupid to have to do it in fourth grade. I thought there had to be more to it. Since Miss Bocachica had encouraged us to use our imagination, I thought maybe Mrs. Fernández wanted to see if I had one too. So I made up a story.

My first picture was the one where the prince kisses the princess, because in my story she told him she was tired; he kissed her, she fell asleep, then woke up, saw the spindle, and began to spin the wool.

I didn't explain any of this to Mrs. Fernández. Instead I showed her the pictures. She raised an eyebrow the way a movie star would. "Let's try another story."

She gave me *Cinderella*.

I made up another story.

When I finished arranging my pictures, I proudly showed them to her.

Mami rested her forehead on her hand.

Turning to Mami, Mrs. Fernández said, "She doesn't know how to arrange pictures in a sequence."

I'd blown it! I thought I had to go back to Cordero, so I began to cry.

"Don't cry," Mrs. Fernández said. "I just don't

understand what you're doing. Tell me why you did this."

Pointing at each picture, I told her that here Cinderella lost her shoe because it was too big on her. Here she and her sisters went to the shoe store. Here a young salesman brought her shoes that fit. The man and Cinderella liked each other, so they went dancing.

Mrs. Fernández smiled. "Hmm! That's *your* story. What about the traditional *Cinderella,* you know, the one most people tell? How would you arrange the pictures?"

"This way." I arranged them quickly.

Mami sighed.

Mrs. Fernández brought out the pictures of *Sleeping Beauty* again. "Very good! What about this one?"

I arranged them in the order she wanted.

"You know how to do it. You just didn't want to." She turned to Mami. "I'm going to pass her, but she might run into problems if she's too different here. Encourage her to do things the way the other girls at La Academia do them, or she won't fit in."

Mrs. Fernández didn't ask about my arithmetic or reading. She seemed more interested in collecting Mami's money for registration and books.

Mami flipped the pages of the red social studies book. "They use this book at Cordero, but Teresa's is green."

"That's last year's edition," Mrs. Fernández said.

"But it's the same."

"Some words are different. And again, if you want Teresa to fit in at La Academia, she has to have the newest edition."

"I understand. I understand." Mami wrote the check. "Can Teresa come without a uniform for a few days until I make her one?"

"Sorry. Carmen Cruz sews our uniforms, and you have to buy them from her. You also have to buy the Buster Brown shoes from La Gloria. "

When we got out of La Academia, Mami told me, "We're going to buy *one* uniform from Doña Carmen, I'll copy her pattern, and I'll make you the rest."

But when we went to buy the uniform, Doña Carmen said to Mami, "You're a better seamstress than I am. I'll tell you what. If you take these blouses home and sew these pleats for me, you won't have to pay for Teresa's uniform and I will pay you."

I felt like hugging Doña Carmen.

I tried on a uniform she'd sewn for a girl who grew too much in the summer.

"You'll have to take it in a quarter of an inch over here," Doña Carmen told Mami, pinching the uniform's white sleeve. "Other than that, I think it fits her. What do you think?"

Mami agreed.

After we finished with the uniform, we went to La Gloria, where we also had luck. The owner was one of Papi's customers. Mami asked him in a whisper if he could sell her the shoes cheaper.

"I can sell you samples," he whispered back. "But they're in the window, and they're a little faded."

Mami and I went to the window and took a peek at the shoes. They looked like boys' shoes. They were brown and had laces.

"Polish can hide anything," Mami said, taking me back inside.

The shoes were a half size too big, but Mami said, "That's good. It'll leave you room to grow."

Mami also bought me a comb. "This is for you to keep those curls in control."

At dinnertime, she told Papi about our day. "We got a free uniform, and let me tell you about the bargain we got at La Gloria." He stayed quiet throughout, but she didn't tell him about my test or about having to buy a new copy of the social studies book.

She also called Doña Carlota and told her that I'd be at La Academia the next day. Mami told me that Marisol was looking forward to seeing me there. Then she sent me to bed—early.

I went to my bedroom but not to bed. I tried on the pleated navy-blue skirt and the vest and bow tie that went with it. I'd never had a skirt with a pocket. I slipped my comb into it.

I didn't try the shoes. I hated those shoes, though Mami had polished them.

I took the uniform off, put on my baby-doll pajamas, went to bed, then got up and tried the uniform on one more time.

I twirled around, making the pleated skirt swing open like an umbrella. This made me remember Miss Bocachica's wedding, the way Ana and I had twirled and danced. I wondered if Ana, Cesar, and Linda had played tag today, if they had missed me. Or maybe they talked about me—how I'd lied and ran away.

"*¡Puf!* Phooey on Ana and her friends!" I twirled again. "Tomorrow I'll be an Academia girl, and I'll have things Ana won't ever have."

12

The next day, after Mami left me in the office at La Academia, the secretary took me down the hallway. I didn't like it there. All the doors were closed, and the hallway was dark. But I couldn't go back to Cordero. Miss Bocachica wasn't there. Ana was, but she hadn't called, and that said it all. I told myself that I didn't want her to call, that I didn't want to be her friend, that I didn't want to see her or anyone in that class ever again. I also told myself that I didn't want to be in a school with rough boys like Cesar who pushed girls into the mud. Cordero definitely wasn't a school for a girl like me, because I was better than they were. Better! No, I didn't want to see them—not after my lying.

As I entered the fourth-grade classroom, I understood why the doors were closed. The classrooms also had air-conditioning. The teacher, who looked old to me, introduced herself as Mrs. Pérez and told me that, since I knew Marisol, I could sit behind her. Marisol smiled at me when I passed by her. I felt the other girls watching me, but I tried not to pay attention to them. They were as white as Marisol. New or not, I would always stand out among these girls, like a pigeon bean in a bag full of white rice.

I sat down. No more wooden desks. These were made out of metal. Cold metal. The blackboards were not black, but green, and there were lots of them—two on a side wall, three on the front wall.

Mrs. Pérez finished talking to the secretary and came to the center of the room. "Girls, as you know, we have a new student."

Her hands, spotted like bananas beginning to get ripe, signaled me to stand up. I did, resting my right knee on the seat and slipping my hand in my skirt pocket, touching my comb.

"Please, stand up straight and introduce yourself," Mrs. Pérez said.

I took my hand out of my pocket and stood straight. The Buster Brown shoes hurt the tops of my feet. Those shoes were *so* heavy.

"My name is Teresa Giraux."

Although the classroom had plenty of light, I felt as if on stage, with the audience watching from the dark.

"Teresa, please tell the class what school you went to," Mrs. Pérez asked.

"I went to Cordero School."

"Where's that?" one of the girls asked.

"It's a small school on Luna Street," Mrs. Pérez said, though Cordero had more students than La Academia.

"Is it private?" This other girl had long, silky, straight hair, like Mami's—except Mami never let hers down like this girl did.

"It is," I answered.

"Who was your teacher?" Mrs. Pérez asked.

"Miss Bocachica."

The theater lights seemed to have come on. The audience applauded and laughed. I burst out laughing too, a nervous laugh. I'd always become angry when somebody laughed at my teacher's name. Bocachica, *boca chica,* small mouth. A funny name. But it was my dear teacher's name, and I didn't like it when they laughed.

My dear teacher. She had written twice. She wanted to know if I'd learned to like Mrs. Ortega. Miss Bocachica didn't know I was at La Academia, wondering what I was doing there. I couldn't write to her. What would I say? That I'd changed schools because of a lie?

Mrs. Pérez asked the girls to introduce themselves. "Giraux," the girl with long, straight hair said. I thought she'd called me by my last name because it was fancy, but at the same time, it shocked me. Ana and Marisol called me "Tere," and here was this girl calling me by my last name. It didn't sound friendly.

"I am Catrina Colón Catalán. But I write my name with *K*s. Katrina Kolón Katalán." She lifted her white-paper finger and wrote the *K*s on the air. No way I could ever forget that name.

I also learned right away the names of two other girls. Olga, who had a cute nose like Ana's. And Eva, who had a gap between her two front teeth.

When the recess bell rang, Marisol held my hand and took me to the hallway. Olga, Eva, and Katrina followed us.

"Does Miss Bocachica have a small mouth?" Marisol asked me.

I nodded.

"How small?" Eva asked in a friendly way, showing the gap between her teeth. "Tiny-tiny?"

"No, it can't be that small." Olga seemed friendly too. "If it was that small, her last name would be *Bocachiquitita.*"

They laughed, but I didn't feel as bad as I felt in the classroom—until Katrina poked my back. I turned to look at her.

"Do you know how to play dodge ball?"

I nodded. "But I don't like it." Last year Linda, Cesar, Ana, and I had played dodge ball. Trying to avoid being hit with the beanbag, I'd run into the Cordero iron fence. I got a bruise on my forehead, and Mami got angry because she thought Miss Bocachica wasn't supervising us enough. I never played dodge ball again.

"Why don't you like it?" Katrina insisted.

I shrugged. "I just don't."

"What did you used to play at recess?" Marisol asked.

We were outside now, and I squinted. The sun made Marisol's hair shine like a new penny.

"We talked and played games on the grass." I didn't want to say we played games in the mud. "No offense, but we didn't grow concrete like you do here." I said that because most of La Academia's patio was covered with concrete.

"We do grow concrete, don't we?" Olga wrinkled her nose, reminding me of Ana. "So, what kind of games did you play at Cordero School?"

"Tag. Passport."

"Passport?" Eva asked. "What's that?"

I swallowed, remembering Miss Bocachica's words teaching us how to play passport. "It's like musical chairs without the chairs. You just assign bases and give them the names of different countries." Katrina frowned, but I continued. "The person in the center calls a country and runs to it. All the other players change countries. The person left without a country goes to the center, and the game starts again."

"It might be fun," Marisol said. "Let's play it."

She took a piece of chalk out of her pocket— probably the same chalk she was using to solve an arithmetic problem on the board when the recess bell rang. She gave me the chalk without saying anything, but I knew she wanted me to use it to write down the bases. I wrote Puerto Rico on the pavement and told her, "You can be here."

I took a few steps and wrote Mexico down. "Olga, here."

Then I called Eva. "You can be Australia."

Katrina had stayed by the only tree in the school patio, a tree with limpy leaves that gave no shade— so different from our níspero tree. I called her. "How would you like to be Japan?"

She tossed her hair back. "Giraux," she yelled, "I don't play baby games."

That startled me, but I decided to ignore her and play with the other girls.

"I want a passport. I want a passport," I called. "I want a passport to Mexico!"

I ran to Mexico. Marisol ran to Australia. Eva and Olga ran to Puerto Rico, but Olga had touched the base first. Eva was It.

Katrina stood still, watching us with her arms folded and making faces every time we laughed. After Eva, Marisol, then Olga became It. She was about to start when two older girls, who had been watching the game, came to me. "Could we play?" one of them asked.

"Sure," I said.

Then Katrina came.

"Would you like to play?" I asked her.

She shrugged.

I assigned the older girls to Brazil and the United States, and Katrina to Japan.

Olga called, "I want a passport. Passport. Passport. To Australia!"

I almost crashed into Marisol, but made it to Puerto Rico. Marisol made it to Brazil. When Katrina made it to the United States, she held on to a pole and laughed, her hair dancing.

By the time the bell rang, more girls had joined us. I'd assigned bases for Costa Rica, India, and El Congo. I'd conquered the world of La Academia!

# 13

*I* had missed Ana, Miss Bocachica, and the other Cordero people on and off almost every day. But I missed them most the day when Mrs. Pérez asked each of us—La Academia girls—to read aloud a paragraph from *My Fourth-Grade English Book*. She hadn't done this since I'd been there. She began with Olga, who sat at the left front corner. I sat close to the door, in the second seat of the farthest right row.

Olga read the paragraph so fast, she lost me. Next Mrs. Pérez called Flor, who sat behind Olga. Flor read the next paragraph with a heavy Spanish accent, but fast, too. I couldn't read that fast, especially not in English. I tried to tell myself what Miss Bocachica used to tell me, that it was okay to read slowly as long as I enjoyed it. But I doubted that worked here.

I prayed for the bell to ring before my turn, but there were forty minutes left of class. I counted the girls who hadn't read, row by row, front to back. Then I counted the paragraphs, until it came to the one I'd have to read. I practiced it many times, without noticing who was reading, without noticing that in our row Mrs. Pérez didn't go front to back, but back to front.

Rebeca was behind me, but I was practicing so hard, I didn't hear her read. She tapped my back, then I heard Mrs. Pérez saying, "Teresa, it's your turn."

I began to read—not too fast, not too slowly.

Marisol, who sat in front of me, turned around and tried to turn my page to the next one. I held the page tight. I couldn't understand what she was doing and why the girls were giggling when I was reading so well.

"Teresa!" Mrs. Pérez called. "You haven't been paying attention. Marisol, show her where we are."

I swallowed hard as Marisol turned the page for me and pointed to the third paragraph. The girls kept giggling, and my ears felt as hot as burners on HI. But I read. Slow-ly. Mrs. Pérez seemed impatient. She finished most words for me. Miss Bocachica would have never done that!

At recess, Mrs. Pérez called me to her desk and told me that I had to work on my reading, that I had to read every day aloud to my parents. I just nodded.

When I left the room, I found Eva, Olga, and Marisol waiting for me.

"What did Mrs. Pérez tell you?" Marisol asked, walking me toward the door to the school patio.

I was about to answer when Katrina, who had been drinking water from the water cooler, jumped in. "Do you always stutter like that when you read?"

"I don . . . don't stutter."

"Ha! You just did."

Katrina opened the door to the school patio and

went out with Olga and Eva, the three of them giggling. Marisol and I stayed in. I leaned on a wall and stared down at the floor, my tears dripping on my Buster Brown shoes. I'd never felt so stupid. I'd never felt so lonely. At Cordero nobody had ever laughed when I read, nobody had ever told me that I stuttered.

"Don't cry," Marisol said. "Sometimes Katrina gets that way."

"She's mean! Why are you her friend?"

"Because we've been together since kindergarten and because her parents and my parents are good friends."

I shook my head, wiping off a tear. "I didn't know I stutter."

"You don't stutter. Katrina is making that up. Come on, let's buy chips."

It was then I realized that Marisol had chosen me over Katrina, that she had not gone to play with Katrina. That felt good. But that afternoon Doña Carlota came in her Cadillac to pick up Marisol, and Katrina went with them.

Marisol saw me but didn't wave good-bye.

*I* worried that Marisol had chosen Katrina over me. But the next day, Saturday, Marisol called me. "Would you like to go swimming at El Escorial?"

"Let me ask Mami!"

Very excited, I ran downstairs to Papi's shop where Mami was hemming a dress and talking to Papi, who had his head under the hood of a car.

"Mami," I interrupted. "Marisol is inviting me to swim at El Escorial. I really want to go. Can I?"

"El Escorial! Do you hear, Ramón? Our daughter has been invited to *El Club Escorial de Ponce.*"

Papi looked out from under the hood and said nothing.

"Ask Marisol when you have to be there," Mami said.

I didn't want Mami to take me to El Escorial in our old car and let other girls see it. So I asked Marisol if her mother could pick me up.

༄

"I'm going to drop the girls at El Escorial," Doña Carlota told Mami when they came to pick me up. "I'll bring them home around three. All right?"

"Fine," Mami answered, which surprised me,

because she never left me anywhere without a grown-up.

On the way to the club Doña Carlota turned the steering wheel gently because the red polish on her long nails wasn't dry. Maybe that was why she didn't smoke on the way. But the car ashtray had lots of cigarette butts ringed with lipstick.

"Teresa," she said, looking at me in the rear-view mirror. "You probably won't see any of the other Academia girls at the club, because most of them are at ballet today."

"Isn't that great?" Marisol said from the front seat. "We won't see Katrina."

"Marisol!" Her mother squeezed her arm. "I told you yesterday that I don't want to hear any of this garbage. You and Katrina have been friends for many years, and I want you to keep it that way."

That told me that, the day before, Marisol had not chosen Katrina over me. She was Katrina's friend mostly because Doña Carlota made her.

"Well, Katrina is so stuck up," Marisol cried. "She thinks it's such a big deal to be the daughter of the president of El Escorial."

"It *is* a big deal!" Marisol's mother said.

"I don't care. The point is that she's a spoiled brat!" Marisol opened and closed her power window. "Nobody dares tell her how spoiled she is, but one of these days I will."

Doña Carlota gave her a stern look. "You're *not* telling her such a thing."

I felt relieved knowing that Marisol didn't like Katrina that much, but I also felt weird because Marisol and her mother were quiet for a long time. As soon as I had something to say, I said it. "Why aren't you taking ballet?"

"I hate it! You have to put your feet like this." Marisol raised her feet and made a *V* with them. "And like this." She made an *L*. "I prefer swimming."

We were now at the club's entrance. The guard peeped in the car window, then opened the gate and waved. Most lawns in Ponce were brown. Here, the grass was green and perfectly cut. Doña Carlota stopped by a tree with purple orchids attached to its trunk. She kissed Marisol and winked at me. "Have fun!"

Marisol and I waved good-bye.

"Let's cross through the dancing hall." Marisol grabbed my hand. "I want you to see it."

It was something to see. The ceilings had paintings of people dancing and kissing and eating and drinking. The terrazzo floors and the stairway railings were so shiny, I could see myself in them. Except in the movies, I'd never seen bathrooms with maids who gave people towels to dry their hands with. El Escorial not only had maids in their bathrooms, but also in the swimming pool dressing rooms.

Marisol gave her Minnie Mouse watch to a maid, who put it away in a locker. Katrina also had a watch like that. Both watches had red bands. And in both, Minnie Mouse wore a red skirt with white polka dots, a red hat with a flower, yellow gloves, and yellow shoes too big for her. Her fingers pointed at the time. I would have done anything for a watch like that.

Although everything else at El Escorial was big, the dressing rooms were too small for two people. "Go ahead and change in that room," Marisol said. "I'll be in the next."

I thought maybe they'd built small rooms for everybody to have their own. I wished Ana and the other Cordero children could see me now among all this wealth. That revenge feeling turned into a more gentle one because I also wanted Ana to enjoy all this. For a minute I thought I'd tell her soon, then I shook my head. No way I'd see Ana. She was gone from my life, and I had to get used to it.

When I came out of my dressing room, I saw Marisol standing by a mirror tying her swimsuit straps at the back of her neck. She wore a two-piece suit. Her legs were the same color as the porcelain angels in church.

I felt bad wearing my one piece. It had a stupid skirt, and my brown legs stuck out like toothpicks. Abuelita was right. I had to eat more.

"This way."

I followed Marisol, feeling my dry, knobby knees bump against each other.

"Are you entering the carnival pageant?" I asked her while we were washing our feet in a shallow pool with a strong chlorine smell.

"No."

"Why not? You would win if you do."

"I don't like that kind of thing."

"How come?" I insisted. "Don't you like wearing a gown and all that?"

Marisol shrugged. "I wear a new gown every year. It's not a big deal."

"It's not just the gown. It's . . . it's more than that." I didn't know what the "more than that" was. But I wanted to wear a gown and be queen!

"Are you entering the pageant?" Marisol asked as if reading my mind.

"I think so."

"It's not going to be easy, Tere," Marisol said, walking toward the big pool. "Katrina also wants to be queen."

"So what? That's not going to stop me." But somehow I thought it was stopping Marisol. "Is Katrina the reason why you won't enter the contest?"

"No! I just like to do other things, like swimming!"

Marisol dived into the big pool. She disappeared, then came up on the other side. "Jump in!"

I dived in and swam to her like a torpedo.

"You're a good swimmer. Do you take private lessons?"

"Every summer." Papi taught Ana and me at Las Cucharas Beach. He didn't have any other students, so they were private lessons.

Marisol and I swam for a while, then sat on lawn chairs to dry and warm up.

"I wish I could get a tan like yours," Marisol said,

studying my arms and legs. "But if I stay in the sun too long, I get as red as a tomato."

I wanted to say that she probably looked cute with pink cheeks. Instead I said, "Marisol, this isn't a suntan. This is the way I am all the time, and I don't like it, because nobody else in our classroom is so dark."

"Well, I think you look pretty."

La Academia had one or two dark kindergartners, and a dark girl who was probably in third grade. Nobody as dark as Nora, though—except for Jeanette Simpson, an American who was in eighth grade. Marisol sometimes practiced English with her.

What I didn't tell Marisol was that, after a few hours at Las Cucharas Beach, my skin got almost as dark as Jeanette's . . . like Ana's. So I couldn't stay in the sun for too long either, especially if I wanted to be carnival queen.

"You know," Marisol said as if reading my mind again, "I saw in a *Vanidades* magazine a woman who squeezed lemon juice on her skin and sat out in the sun to get whiter."

I laughed. "Did it work?"

"I don't know. Let's try it!"

Marisol sprang from her chair, ran to the pool bar, and came back with her cupped hands full with half lemons. She squeezed the lemon juice on my legs, and it got into a couple of fresh mosquito bites. "It stings!" I jumped in the pool and rubbed my legs, but the chlorine didn't help. I rushed out and ran to the shower.

~~~~

Soon Marisol came. "I'm sorry."

"It's okay," I said, my legs red from all the rubbing. "It's better now."

"I'm hungry, are you?"

I said I was.

After the shower we got dressed and went to the club restaurant. The large room faced an interior patio with a well in the middle that had purple and orange *trinitaria* vines growing on its side posts. The *trinitarias* reminded me of the Cordero School entrance, but these were even prettier, I decided.

We sat at a table close to them.

"Would you ladies like fresh fruit punch?" the waiter asked.

"Yes, please," Marisol said.

He served us the fruit punch and left the pitcher on the table. "Today," he said, "you have the choice of lobster sandwiches, breaded shrimp, or veal parmigiana. Would you like some time to decide?"

Marisol nodded.

I whispered, "I brought only one dollar."

"Ah, don't worry about money. I sign the bill, and my parents pay it at the end of the month."

"Is that okay with your parents?"

"Sure."

"What are you having?" I asked.

"Breaded shrimp. I love them with tartar sauce."

"I want that too." What else could I say? Lobster sandwiches sounded way too fancy, and I'd never heard of that other dish.

When the waiter came, Marisol ordered for both of us. He asked if I wanted my shrimp with cole slaw salad. I nodded, though I didn't know what cole slaw was.

When he brought it, I loved its sweet flavor.

"I really like it here," I told Marisol.

"Tell your parents to become members."

If we belonged to the club, I could wear a carnival gown—even if I wasn't queen. But I knew that Mami and Papi couldn't afford the membership fee. Yet I didn't want to tell this to Marisol. I shook my head and giggled nervously.

"Why not?" Marisol asked.

I shrugged, thinking that maybe I could give it a try. Maybe Mami could persuade Papi. "Yes, why not."

∽

"Why not!" Papi said later. "Do you know how much it costs to be a member of El Escorial? At least sixty dollars a month, and that's without the registration fee."

"We should make the sacrifice, Ramón."

"You're getting crazy, Dolores. We can't afford that. I already repair cars day and night to buy her books. You sew all day to pay half of her tuition. This is crazy. We're not rich, Dolores. No! We're not joining El Escorial!"

Papi took his comb out and combed his hair. Then, out of the blue, he said, "And, Teresa, I want to know why you aren't Ana's friend anymore."

"Ramón." Mami jumped in. "They're not friends because they're not in the same school. That's the way girls are."

I wanted to have a better reason for not being Ana's friend, one that I could tell Papi. I didn't find any. I turned around and looked outside. A girl I didn't know stared at me from an old, rusted car. I stuck my tongue out at her.

## 15

When I told my parents that I wanted to be in the carnival pageant, Papi said nothing, but Mami encouraged me. "You would have to compete in a talent show, you know? What do you plan to do?"

"I'll read."

Mami glanced at Papi, then she said to me, "Teresa, you'd be better off singing or dancing or even reciting. But reading?"

"It's going to be okay, Mami. I'll be reading something I wrote at Cordero."

I'd decided to read the *coquí* composition. I thought I'd win if I did.

"Why don't you practice reading it to us?" Papi said.

"I won't need to."

Papi and Mami gave each other sad looks.

"Don't worry," I told them. "I'll do fine."

There were two steps to the Ponce carnival pageant. Each school had a talent show in which fourth-grade girls with fairly good grades could participate. The judges of that contest chose one or two winners, who then went to a citywide competition in which three were chosen—a queen, a princess, and a runner-up.

The day of La Academia's pageant, I felt I could win. I'd read my composition aloud to myself many times, and I could read it well.

Only Katrina, Eva, Olga, and I were going to be in the pageant. Marisol didn't want to be in it. Flor did, but her grades were lousy. Rebeca also wanted to enter the contest. But she didn't—Katrina had told her that she couldn't dance because *she,* Katrina Kolón Katalán, was dancing.

Katrina's mother came earlier to school and helped Katrina change into a fluffy yellow-and-black tutu. She curled Katrina's hair and tied it into a bouncy ponytail. Katrina looked prettier than any of the famous ballet dancers I'd seen on TV.

I was wearing my pique dress, the only dress Mami had made me that didn't have a bow in back. I'd persuaded Mami to let me wear my patent-leather shoes without socks. But now I knew the importance of wearing socks. Walking to school, I'd gotten blisters on my heels.

Olga and Eva were wearing nice dresses, but nothing very fancy. So, blisters and all, I felt good about myself.

Mrs. Pérez sat us in chairs on La Academia's stage, and she went to sit at the judges' table below with Principal Fernández, the secretary, Marisol's mother, and the mayor. The rest of the girls were sitting out there in the auditorium. I thought I could see Marisol's red hair, but the bright stage lights were on, and all I could really see were silhouettes. Mami also sat somewhere out there.

The first contestant, Olga, recited a poem so fast, nobody could understand it. The audience hardly applauded, but she shrugged as if she didn't care if she'd lost.

Katrina walked to the middle of the stage and took her position, her arms behind her back like the wings of a resting butterfly. The stage lights turned blue, and she began to dance. On the tips of her ballet shoes, she took tiny steps in place, her head down as if teasing a flower. Then she flew to the middle of the stage—and fell!

Everybody gasped! The white stage lights went on and, within seconds, Katrina's parents were walking her off the stage. Katrina seemed to be all right, but she was crying. Before she left the stage, she kicked my chair—as if her fall had been my fault.

It was my turn. Or at least that was what Mrs. Fernández said while moving the microphone to the center of the stage. I stood up and began to read.

"The coquí is . . . a tree . . . "

My hands and voice were trembling.

". . . a tree-frog that sings all night . . . "

I could see the judges. Mrs. Fernández was with Katrina's parents consoling Katrina by the side of the stage. But Doña Carlota, the secretary, Mrs. Pérez, and the mayor were listening. I could tell that Mrs. Pérez didn't like my reading because she kept shaking her head and making faces.

". . . and when . . . when it rains . . .

Katrina's father came to talk to the mayor, and the mayor and Mrs. Pérez stepped to the side to talk to him. Doña Carlota and the secretary were the only ones listening to me, but I kept reading, now more smoothly, until I finished. Some people applauded—Mami maybe, Marisol for sure, and maybe others who listened because they couldn't see what was going on with Katrina.

I sat down, knowing I'd lost. I wanted to cry, but somehow I couldn't. My throat felt as if I'd swallowed in all those words I'd just said, and now they were stuck between my mouth and my heart.

The judges had a short meeting.

Eva waited until they were all back in their seats before she began to sing. I got angry at myself. I could have done the same thing, wait for the judges to be in their seats.

"*Verde luz de monte y mar,* green light on the hill and on the sea . . . " Eva sang, her voice as delicate as a glass bell. She would certainly win. But who would be the other girl? The judges would have to choose between Olga, Katrina, and me. I'd done better than the two of them. I swallowed the lump in my throat and sat straight, more sure of myself.

The audience gave Eva a huge applause.

Then Mrs. Fernández came on to the stage. "As you know, Katrina fell," she said. "She fell because she's not used to dancing on a stage with all these chairs. We're going to remove them, and she'll dance for us again."

That made sense to me. It had to be hard to dance with those chairs around. But why give Katrina a second chance and not give me one? After all, some of the judges were not listening when I read. But did I really want a second chance? No, I didn't want to go through that again.

After we were taken off the stage and the chairs were moved, Katrina came in, dancing. On the tips of her ballet shoes, she took tiny steps in place, her arms flapping like butterfly wings, her head down as if teasing a flower. She went from place to place, from flower to flower. Then she flew to the middle of the stage and threw her arms up into an arch, bent the top of her body back, and turned around thanking God for the flowers and their nectar. She flew to the flowers and teased them once more until she found the right flower. She stopped long enough to sip its nectar, taking tiny steps, and fluttering her hands gently back and forth. Then she flew to the middle of the stage where she turned and turned and turned. Very pretty!

Everybody applauded a lot.

After Katrina had bowed over and over again, Mrs. Fernández took us back up to the stage. "This is the big moment," she said.

It wasn't such a big moment. Everybody knew who had won.

Still, I sighed when Mrs. Fernández announced, "In fourth place is Olga Oliver." At least I wasn't in last place.

"In third place, Teresa Giraux."

The mayor gave me a blue ribbon and shook my hand. Olga got a green ribbon.

"In second place and silver ribbon, Eva Solás! And

our winner and for sure Carnival Queen of Ponce, Katrina Kolón Katalán!"

It didn't take long for the stage to get full of people congratulating Katrina. I stayed in place, my tears making circles on my ribbon. Now I had no chance to wear a gown.

I saw Doña Carlota's high-heeled sandals in front of me. She hugged me. "I'm sorry," she whispered in my ear. "I tried to persuade the judges to give you a second chance, but Mrs. Pérez said you always get nervous when you read, and she didn't want to put you through it one more time."

I nodded. "It's okay."

I rushed down and looked for Mami, who was standing in the back of the auditorium. I clutched her by the waist, crying.

"Let's go." With her arm on my shoulder, Mami took me out of there.

I expected her to scold me because I didn't practice reading the poem with her, but as soon as we stepped out of La Academia, she said, "That wasn't fair."

"But," I sobbed, "Katrina danced well . . . "

"She did, but she had a second chance. You deserved another chance too. Let's go shopping. I'll buy you a little something."

We walked to Atocha Street, where most of the stores were. I said no to everything Mami suggested until we walked in front of the window of Bonita Fashions.

"I want that dress to go to Marisol's birthday party." If I couldn't have a gown, maybe I could have a less expensive dress.

Mami kept on walking. "I can make you one."

I stayed there. "Could I have that one?"

Mami walked back and read the price. Thirty dollars. Mami opened her purse and took out her checkbook. I thought she wanted to see how much money she had, but instead she began to draw. On the back of a check stub she drew the orange sweetheart blouse with turquoise fish designs and the thick, turquoise polyester skirt.

"Don't worry," she said. "It's going to look just like that."

We went to another store and bought enough fabric to make two dresses—one for me and one to give Marisol as a birthday gift. I wanted to give Marisol a bracelet with a charm I'd seen in a jewelry store. But the fabric for both dresses cost only six dollars.

# 16

*T*he girls at La Academia were not talking about what to wear for Marisol's birthday party. Instead they talked about their carnival gowns. Miriam Chandri was designing Olga's guava gown. Fernando Pena, Eva's mango one. Carlota Alfaro, Katrina's pineapple. All of them were famous designers who lived in San Juan, the largest city and capital of Puerto Rico.

"Marisol, why didn't you choose a San Juan designer?" Katrina asked, standing by the side chalkboard and peering at me.

"Well," Marisol answered, "it doesn't make sense to pay a San Juan designer when we have a fine one right here in Ponce."

I smiled not only because I liked what she'd just said, but also because I knew those were her mother's words.

"What does your gown look like?" Katrina asked Marisol after glancing at Mrs. Pérez, who was sitting at her desk.

"I'll tell you if you tell me what yours looks like," Marisol said.

"No, it's a surprise."

"Well, Katrina, so is mine."

"What about yours, Giraux? Is it a surprise too?"

I didn't want to say that I couldn't go to the carnival because I wasn't a member of El Escorial. Instead I said, "My mother hasn't designed it yet."

Mrs. Pérez raised her head from the papers she was grading. "She hasn't?"

I shook my head.

"Call your mother and tell her to come to talk to me this afternoon."

After school Mami and I went to the classroom, where Mrs. Pérez explained to us that the whole class had to represent Puerto Rican fruits at the El Escorial carnival in February. "They have to be there, Señora Giraux."

"But we're not members of El Escorial," Mami whispered, though nobody else was in the classroom.

"That's something else I want to talk about," Mrs. Pérez said. "We're not supposed to pressure you. But Mrs. Fernández and I think that Teresa will fit in better among the girls if you become members of El Escorial."

I felt like jumping up and down. I wanted to be a full high-society girl. For that, I not only needed to have a bunch of things, be an Academia girl, and be white. I also had to be a member of El Escorial, I decided, remembering the club's swimming pool, its restaurant, its dancing hall—and the gown I could wear.

"Think about it, Señora Giraux. Teresa can be in the carnival, but you won't be able to go unless you're members. All the other parents will be there."

All that worry for nothing. I could be in the carnival and wear a gown. Mami and Papi were the ones who couldn't go. Still, I wanted to be a member of El Escorial.

Mami didn't agree to anything in front of Mrs. Pérez, but on the way home she said, "Teresa, we're going to be members of El Escorial. I'll send the application and won't tell your father until the membership letter arrives."

"*¡Chévere!*" I said, without thinking that we were betraying Papi.

When we got home, Papi gave me a letter from Miss Bocachica. I went to my bedroom to read it. The letter was written in Spanish, but it said:

> *Ana wrote saying that you changed schools. If your parents transferred you, I'm sure they had a good reason. But Ana also told me that the two of you are not friends anymore. That makes me very sad. I'm writing to Ana asking her, as I'm asking you, to please try to be friends again. Do it for me.*

I took the letter to the hallway and dialed Ana's phone number. Ana answered, "Hello."

I covered the phone's mouthpiece and didn't say anything.

"Hello. Hellooo."

It was nice to hear Ana's voice. But I didn't say anything, and she hung up. Slowly, I did too.

It wasn't that easy. For me to be Ana's friend, I had to apologize. And that was hard!

The phone rang, startling me. Somehow I expected to hear Ana's voice. Instead I heard Marisol—inviting me to go to her house the following day.

"Let me ask my parents, and I'll call you back."

∽

I found Mami and Papi in the sewing room, where Mami was getting ready to sew the green velvet for Marisol's gown.

"Marisol wants to know if I can go to her house tomorrow."

"Teresa." Mami lifted her foot from the sewing-machine pedal. "Tomorrow we're going to Coamo. You need to go with us because you haven't visited Buelo, Buela, and Abuelita in ages."

"Can I invite Marisol to Coamo?"

"No!" Mami said.

"Why not?" Papi asked.

I almost answered, "Because Abuelita doesn't have teeth," but Mami jumped in. "Come on, Ramón, I'm not going to introduce Marisol to my toothless mother and show her where she lives."

"Why not? It would be good for Marisol to see how other people are, how other people live."

"Forget it, Ramón Giraux. I won't humiliate Teresa and myself by doing such a thing."

"Humiliate? You mean that you feel humiliated by your own mother?"

"By her teeth and by how she lives, Ramón!"

Papi shook his head. "Dolores, Dolores."

I'd never felt humiliated by how Abuelita lived—

although maybe I should have. After all, Abuelita didn't live any better than Ana. That made me ask, "Why didn't you let me take Ana to Coamo? It wasn't because of the way Abuelita lives, was it?" No answer. "Was it because Abuelita has no teeth?"

"No, Teresa," Mami said. "But what does Ana have to do with this?"

"Then it's because Ana is black, isn't it?"

"You got it!" Papi said.

"Ramón!"

"She was going to know sooner or later."

Mami shook her head, but then said, "Teresa, the truth is that Abuelita would have a hard time if she knew that you have a black friend." Mami stared down at the fabric on her sewing machine. "Abuelita just wants the best for you."

"Ha!" Papi said.

Mami gave him a stern look. "She does, Ramón!"

Papi opened his mouth to say something, but Mami turned toward me. "Anyway, Teresa, let's talk about Marisol, so you can call her back."

"*Ajá,* let's talk about Marisol," Papi said. "Is it a humiliation to invite her here? We don't live like she lives, you know."

Mami waved him off. "Marisol has seen this place. Teresa, tell her to come today."

"Here?" I asked.

Papi and Mami nodded.

"But what would we play?"

"Dolls," Papi said.

"Dolls! We're too big to play with dolls."

Mami shrugged. "You play with dolls at Marisol's house."

"We just dress them up."

"You can dress up Robertito."

"You don't understand, Mami. Robertito is a baby doll. Marisol doesn't have baby dolls. Her dolls are different. I won't show Robertito to Marisol. I won't! I won't!"

"Okay, okay," Papi said. "What if you play downstairs where the tires are?"

I thought about it. Marisol wouldn't blend in with the dark like Ana did. So I said yes.

◡

As soon as Marisol came, we went to Papi's shop. We jumped from tire to tire and played hide-and-seek in piles five tires high. Marisol loved it. When we got bored, it occurred to me that we could play in the bins of metal nuts and bolts. I didn't suggest it. That was a game I'd played with Ana, and somehow I wanted for it to be just Ana's game. It was silly to think that way when Ana and I were not friends anymore. But I couldn't play it with Marisol.

"Let's go to the Sol de Borinquen," I suggested instead.

As black and dirty as we were, we crossed the street to the bakery to buy *pastelillos de guayaba*, pastries with guava filling.

"Take your fingers off the window display," Don Felipe told Marisol, who was pointing at the *pastelillos*.

Don Felipe didn't say this only because we were dirty. He used to say it to all the children. I wasn't sure he'd dare say it to a grown-up, but everybody who knew he polished the displays all the time stayed away from them.

After Marisol and I paid, we sat on the bakery's front step to eat the *pastelillos*. Our faces got white with powdered sugar, our hands sticky with guava. Marisol studied her hands. She stood up, went to the window where Don Felipe displayed his cakes, and stamped her hands on the glass. I laughed and stamped mine too.

"He's coming!" I yelled when I saw Don Felipe's wrinkled face on the other side of the window.

Marisol and I ran across the street. "He's coming!" I yelled to Marisol when we made it to the house. She climbed the stairs, taking two steps at a time. I did the same, slamming the front door.

We hid in the bathroom.

The doorbell rang, and soon after, Mami called us out. She asked us to apologize to Don Felipe. He accepted our apologies, his wrinkles sagging.

I thought Mami would be so angry that she'd tell me that I couldn't go to the carnival, and I wouldn't have a gown. But when Don Felipe left, she burst out laughing. "Did you see his face? I don't think he knew you girls had it in you!"

I sighed, relieved, but still surprised that Mami wasn't angry. Maybe it was because Marisol did it. What if it had been Ana? Mami had scolded Ana for smaller things than that, like the day Ana tried to stick her fingers in Mami's mouth. . . . Why was Mami like this?

Papi had said that these feelings were learned. Mami must have learned them from Abuelita! Was I learning mine from Mami?

"Tere," Marisol said, shaking my thoughts away, "you know what? It's more fun to play at your house than to play at mine."

I thought about that. Marisol probably had to be ladylike in her fancy house, but here she could get all dirty and have fun. Still, I shook my head. Marisol had no idea how much she had.

**17**

Mrs. Pérez gave each of us a Red Cross card with twenty empty slots to fill with dimes. I'd done this every year at Cordero, where some children returned them with only a few dimes. Miss Bocachica always told us, "Every little bit helps."

I'd always returned mine full. Ana did too, though it was harder for her to get the money. She walked around her neighborhood looking down, hoping to find a dime here or there. If I had extra dimes, I gave them to her to complete her card.

Anyway, for the La Academia card, Mami, Papi, Buelo, Buela, and Abuelita gave me dimes. I hated to ask other people, but I was still short. So when I went with Mami to return some shirts, I asked Doña Carmen. She gave me four dimes, not enough.

I didn't want to ask Don Felipe. I really didn't. But what choice did I have?

When I entered the Sol de Borinquen, he was busy with a customer. I sat on a stool at the soda fountain and went round and round on the red seat until he finally paid attention to me. "Teresa, those seats are not for swiveling."

I stopped, but I didn't believe him. If the seats were not meant for swiveling, why did they swivel?

"Is there something I can do for you?"

I stood up and took the Red Cross card out of my pants pocket.

"Missing five dimes, eh?"

I nodded.

"Okay, I'll help you if you promise me that you won't put your dirty hands on my displays again."

I lowered my eyes. "I promise." Then, without thinking, I swiveled side to side.

"And that you won't break my seats."

I stopped. "I won't."

He went to the cash register and came back with five dimes. I'd started inserting them in their slots when he asked, "Where's your friend?"

"At her house, I guess," I answered, thinking he was talking about Marisol.

"You know," he said, handing me a dime, "she used to come to buy bread, but since you changed schools, she hasn't come anymore."

He was talking about Ana! Why wasn't she coming to the bakery anymore? Maybe it was because the bakery was right in front of my house.

"You're still friends, aren't you?"

I nodded, placing the dime he'd given me in the last slot.

"I hope so. Because she's one of the nicest girls I've ever met . . . nicer than that girl you brought here the other day—who put her dirty hands on my glass."

❧

At the end of the next day I proudly gave my card to Mrs. Pérez like everyone else was doing. But on my way out I saw the girls giving not only the full cards to Mrs. Pérez, but checks with a donation from their parents.

"How much is your check for?" Olga asked Marisol.

"For fifty dollars, and yours?"

"Twenty-five."

Katrina tossed her long silky hair back. "My father gave me a check for one hundred dollars."

Before they could ask me, I ran outside.

I walked home feeling bad because I didn't have enough money to be like the other Academia girls. But when I was about to cross Luna Street, I began to think it wasn't such a big deal. I didn't know the girls were going to take checks. Next year, I thought, I could ask Papi . . . no, I could ask Mami to write a check.

About half a block later I stopped. My social studies book! I'd left it at school. I made an about-face to go back to find it. Then I saw Ana! She was at the corner of Luna and Torre streets. A few minutes before, she hadn't been there.

Cordero, only one and a half blocks away, ended its school day before La Academia. She was probably waiting for her father.

Watching her, I remembered Don Felipe saying that Ana was nicer than Marisol. He didn't know anything!

I jaywalked instead of crossing the street where Ana was skipping. I didn't understand how she could be so happy, especially when she had on *that* uniform. I now believed that loafers were not proper shoes for a uniform, nor was an A-line skirt without pleats, or a blouse without a vest or bow tie. I felt glad I didn't have to wear that uniform anymore, that I was at La Academia among high-society girls.

About to cross the street again, I heard her calling. First it was almost a whisper—"Tere?" as if she wasn't sure I was Tere. Maybe because I looked different wearing my Academia uniform.

Then louder, "Teresa?"

My legs went fast, faster than the legs of a chicken being chased.

Then came an angry call. "Teresa Giraux!"

I ran, ran, ran—all the way to La Academia.

I glanced back, expecting her to be following me—kind of wanting for her to be following me. But I only saw a fruit vendor. I crossed the school patio, wondering what was wrong with me, why I couldn't stop for Ana. But I didn't want to think about her. I had to get my book.

I walked into the classroom and found Katrina sitting at my desk, combing her long, silky hair with my comb.

"Give it!" I said, stretching out my hand.

"Why? Can't you afford another?"

I picked up my book, snatched the comb out of her hand, and rushed out.

"Everybody knows that you only gave two dollars to the Red Cross!"

I hated Katrina! I hated her!

A few days later I began to hate her even more.

I bent to tie my shoe at school, and my hair flipped down.

"Teresa," Eva said, "you have head lice!"

"No I don't." I touched my head, thinking she was kidding. Eva was nice . . . when away from Katrina.

Anyway, I couldn't possibly have head lice. Ana had gotten some once. From Nora, Ana had said. After that, nobody wanted to play with Nora. Those weren't happy times for me either, because Mami called Miss Bocachica and told her she'd keep me home until she could assure her that nobody had lice at school. And I couldn't see Ana.

But that was at Cordero. I couldn't possibly get lice at La Academia.

"*Ajá.*" Eva nodded. "You have lice. I saw the eggs."

She ran to the classroom and told Mrs. Pérez, who sent me straight to the office.

The school secretary checked my head with an ice-cream stick and called Mami. "Teresa has little problems in her hair. You better come to pick her up so we can explain what to do."

While I waited, the whole class marched in to get checked. Only Katrina and I had head lice.

"You gave me lice," she said. "I shouldn't have combed my hair with your dumb comb!"

I felt embarrassed. Then Mami came. She shook her head. I began to cry, but calmed down when the secretary told Mami that lice didn't have anything to do with dirty hair. "People get them from touching heads, wearing other people's hats, using other people's combs."

From using other people's combs! Katrina got them from using my comb, but I still couldn't tell how I got them.

At home Mami followed the secretary's directions strictly. She applied a special shampoo to my dry hair and left it on for a long time. She boiled all our combs and brushes. She put my bed linen in the washing machine, my pillow in a plastic bag, my stuffed animals in the freezer. She also had to listen to Katrina's mother, who called to tell Mami not to send me to school until my head was completely clear. She didn't want Katrina to get lice from me anymore.

"This is humiliating," Mami told me with tears in her eyes. "She even called you *trigueñita,* dark girl."

I also felt humiliated until Marisol phoned. She told me that Katrina's two little sisters had had lice a week ago and that for sure I'd gotten the lice from her. At first I didn't believe Marisol. Then I thought she had to be right because I didn't have lice before Katrina used my comb.

I told Mami, then I said, "I'd always thought that La Academia girls didn't get lice."

Mami pinched her lips, pushed my head back down, and quietly continued pulling out the gelatine-like eggs with a fine-tooth comb. It wasn't until Papi came home that she talked. "We should cut her hair."

I agreed. When I met Marisol, I thought she'd liked my hair. But she never said anything about it.

How could anybody like my curls—except for Papi, who was now saying, "No, Dolores. We can't cut those beautiful curls."

"Cut them! Cut them! Nobody at La Academia has curls like mine. I don't need them."

Papi patted my shoulder. "Don't panic. You just have a few eggs left."

I spent three days at home because Mami kept seeing white stuff in my hair. On the fourth day she took me to school, and the secretary checked my head.

"Señora Giraux, what you see is dandruff. See, it's flaky. You probably tried so hard to get rid of the lice that her scalp got dry."

She sent me to the classroom.

When I went in, I had to look at Katrina twice. She had cut her hair so short, I thought she was a boy. No way she could become queen looking like that.

# 18

The day of the citywide contest Doña Carlota—who was a judge again—drove Katrina, Eva, Marisol, Mrs. Fernández, and Mrs. Pérez to El Teatro La Perla. The rest of us walked to the theater with the secretary.

As soon as we got there, Mrs. Pérez came to steer us away from Maruca, who was cutting paper dolls out of a newspaper page. Maruca made me remember the marshmallow wedding and the candies Ana had bought from him. Mami never got to know that I'd eaten Maruca's candies, but now I knew why she didn't want me to eat them. It wasn't just because Maruca didn't wear shoes, but also because he was black.

We entered the theater and Mrs. Pérez sat us close to the stage. "I prefer to sit in the balcony," I told Marisol, who had been waiting for us.

I looked up and quickly changed my mind. Mrs. Ortega, Cesar, Nora, Luis, Linda's parents, and Ana's parents were in the balcony. That told me that Ana and Linda had won the Cordero contest. Otherwise, their parents wouldn't have been invited.

I didn't want them to see me. So I buried myself in my seat and stayed still, until the lights went off and the contest began.

For this first part the contestants had to read a

poem written in English by themselves. The girl from Morel Campos Public School came to the stage and recited with a really heavy accent:

*"Are you ever a . . . afraid of the spooky owl?*
*Are . . . you ever frightened . . . by . . . by the wolf*
*howl . . . "*

The girl forgot the rest of the poem. People applauded, but I knew she'd lost.

Linda came to the stage. She looked whiter than white, but she introduced herself and recited loudly, almost without an accent.

*"Oh, cat! How I envy you!*
*No work, no worries in your mind*
*or anything of the sort.*
*Just feeling some kind of pleasure*
*in your fantastic mind."*

Her poem made a lot of sense to me, because Linda not only had a cat, she also complained a lot about all the schoolwork she had to do.

Eva's turn.

*"Pandas and bears, eagles and whales*
*Fill our lives with stories and tales."*

Eva had a heavy accent, but something else was wrong with her voice. "Is she hoarse?" I asked Marisol.

Marisol nodded.

"And she's going to sing?"

"She's going to try."

After Eva, Katrina came onto the stage dressed in a blue polyester dress and recited:

*"Up there somewhere there's a place of love.*
*Up there somewhere is the moonlight above.*
*Up there somewhere the sun lights the way.*
*Down here where the air is clear,*
*the horses and birds play."*

A nice poem, I had to admit. But I'd heard it all week because Mrs. Pérez made Katrina practice it a million times until Mrs. Pérez heard no accent.

Finally, it was Ana's turn. She'd always been a great poetry writer, and Miss Bocachica had always encouraged her. She introduced herself and began to recite with an accent but with a lot of expression.

*"Tell me why the insults fly.*
*Tell me why a child must cry.*
*And what is the color of our souls.*
*Is it the color of laughter and love?*
*Is it the hue of a rainbow above?*
*Is it the image we fail to see?*
*Love for mankind is my fantasy."*

Everybody applauded, but I stayed stone still. I knew Ana had written that poem for me, the one who had insulted her; the one who had lied to her; the one who had run away from her.

The lights came on for an intermission.

"Let's go to the bathroom," Marisol said.

I shook my head. "I don't need to go."

Marisol went with Olga, and I stayed. "'Tell me why the insults fly,'" I repeated to myself. "'What is the color of our souls. . . .'" ¡Ay!

After the intermission the student from the Morel Campos School performed a one-person play about a woman who had a really bad stomachache. It was very funny! But unless the others messed up, this girl had no chance of winning, because she'd been the one who had forgotten her poem.

Linda was next. She sang, "*Qué será, será,*" beautifully. People clapped and clapped and clapped.

"Do you know her?" Marisol asked me, clapping.

"I do, but I didn't know she could sing so well."

When Linda had left the stage, Eva came on. She took the microphone, brought it close to her mouth and sang, "*Verde luz . . .*" Her voice sounded like a broken glass bell. When she finished, the audience gave her a polite applause. Eva left the stage crying.

Linda had won. But *what* had she won? Would she be the runner-up, the princess, or the queen?

I expected to see Katrina next, but Ana came to the stage. She was wearing a long skirt with ruffles, and a handkerchief on her head. No way she could win wearing that outfit!

She took the microphone with confidence and began to recite in Spanish Luis Palés Matos's "*Danza negra,* Black Dance."

"*Calabó y bambú.*
"Calabo and bamboo

*Bambú y calabó.*
Bamboo and calabo.

*El gran Cocoroco dice: tu-cu-tú.*
The great Cocoroco says, 'Too-coo-too.'

*La Gran Cocoroca dice: to-co-tó."*
The great Cocoroca says, 'To-co-toe.'"

She moved her hands, hips, and feet to the rhythm of the poem. Everybody began to clap to the same rhythm.

*"Es el sol de hierro que arde en Tombuctú.*
"It's the iron sun that burns in Timbuktu.

*Es la danza negra de Fernando Poo."*
It's the black dance of Fernando Po."

People began to drum the floor with their feet.

*"El cerdo en el fango gruñe: pru-pru-prú.*
"The pig in the mud squeals: *pru-pru-pru.*

*El sapo en la charca sueña: cro-cro-cró.*
The toad in the pond dreams: *cro-cro-crow.*

*Calabó y bambú.*
Calabo and bamboo.

*Bambú y calabó."*
Bamboo and calabo."

Ana lowered her voice and repeated it over and over until nobody could hear her:

~~~~
*131*

*"Calabó y bambú.*

"Calabo and bamboo.

*Bambú y calabó."*

Bamboo and calabo."

"Bravo!" Everybody stood up to clap—everybody except me. Until Marisol pulled me to my feet. "Do you know her?"

"She . . . was in my class."

"She's great! Bravo!"

Ana *was* great! She'd recited a poem nobody could understand and was wearing a terrible African outfit. But *everybody,* including the people from La Academia, had liked her performance. I did too.

"Bravo!" I finally said just before the curtain went down.

They had not used the curtain until now. When it went back up, a butterfly from the heavens came in—dancing. Except that it wasn't a butterfly, but Katrina with short hair. She danced as beautifully as she'd danced at La Academia. Still, Ana was the best!

When Katrina's dance ended, everybody applauded. The curtain came down and up again. Katrina bowed a ballerina bow, and the people applauded harder.

Finally, the mayor came to the stage and asked the other girls to join him. Ana came out and stood with her feet crossed. She didn't have to be nervous. She was queen!

"Our runner-up," the mayor announced, "is Linda Miranda."

He congratulated Linda and gave her a bouquet of daisies. Then he turned to Ana and Katrina. "This is hard because both of these girls did well. But our princess is Ana Montañez . . . Katrina Kolón Katalán is our queen!"

I stood up. Shocked. I shook my head and plopped myself back into the seat. "I can't believe it."

"I can," Marisol said. I gave her a puzzled look, and she added, "Don't forget that Katrina's father has a lot of money."

"What do you mean?"

"Come on, girls," Mrs. Pérez interrupted. "Go up to the stage and congratulate Katrina."

Marisol turned to me. "I'll tell you later."

Going up the stage stairs, I saw Ana coming down. I put my hand on the elbow where the bouquet of roses the mayor had given her rested. "Congratulations," I said, smiling.

She froze, peered at me, then shook my hand off. "Congratulations? Go congratulate Katrina. She's the queen." And she moved on.

I had to keep going because I had people behind me, but I heard Don Toño saying, "Ana! That wasn't very nice."

When I got to the stage, I stood outside the cluster of people congratulating Katrina. Mrs. Pérez pushed me in, but I went back out. I felt angry. Guilty. Sad. Everything at once.

Ana was leaving the theater. I wanted to run to her, take her by the hand and walk her to the stage, yank Katrina out of the throne, and sit Ana there, where she belonged.

But I stayed where I was and did nothing—among the La Academia girls.

## 19

The next day, for Marisol's birthday party, Mami helped me put on the dress she'd made. It turned out to be exactly like the one at Bonita Fashions.

"Do something with those uncontrollable curls, would you?" Mami kissed me. "And have fun—for you and for me."

She wanted to come to the party, but she couldn't. Besides buying sequins for Marisol's carnival gown, she had to finish sewing ten blouses for Doña Carmen and four dresses for other clients.

After she left, I combed my hair into a ponytail so tight it pulled my eyebrows up. I took half of the ponytail, looped it up, and fastened it with bobby pins. I looped the other half down and pinned it too. From the back my hair looked like a wavy *8*.

I was late. Quickly, I wrapped Marisol's dress that Mami had put inside a box, and I hurried down to Papi's shop.

He took one look at me and said, "What have you done to your hair? You look like an iguana."

That made me angry. I sat in the backseat of the car, angry also because I had to be driven in our car that was so old. I stared out the window, avoiding

Papi's eyes in the mirror as he said, "You're a beautiful girl, Teresa. You don't need to imitate other people."

Papi probably thought I was imitating Doña Carlota's beehive, but I wasn't. I just didn't want my hair to look too curly.

"And please," Papi continued, driving up the hill. "Be considerate with your mother. She's working hard to give you what she didn't fully have in her childhood." He glanced at me again. "But she's not a magician. She can't turn cotton into silk. Do you know what I mean?"

I thought I knew what he meant. I'd been asking for too much, but for me to be a high-society girl I needed everything I'd asked for and a Ginny doll and a two-piece swimsuit and a Minnie Mouse watch.

Papi dropped me off at Marisol's and waited until I got in.

Marisol's father opened the door. "So, who's this young lady?"

"Teresa," I said shyly.

I'd not met him before because he traveled a lot, selling and buying land around the island. Yet I knew right away who he was because he looked like Marisol—porcelain skin, red hair, aqua eyes. He had on a white *guayabera* with long sleeves, one of those embroidered shirts Papi had said a million times he liked but couldn't afford.

He waved at Papi, who waved back and left.

"Aren't your parents coming?"

Marisol had invited all ten girls in our class and

their families. But when we got the invitation, Papi joked that he couldn't go because they didn't make a brush thin enough for him to wash the grease out from under his nails. And Mami had no time.

I finally answered Marisol's father's question. "They are too busy."

"That's too bad."

He took me to the terrace, where an orchestra was playing a *bolero*. Marisol came to me, beautiful in the lilac taffeta dress Mami had made her. We kissed each other's cheeks, then she pinned a *capia* on my shoulder. It had a tiny photograph of her. Ha! At Miss Bocachica's wedding Mami had said that people didn't give *capias* at parties anymore. And here was high, high-society Marisol giving them. How wrong Mami was!

I gave Marisol the gift, and she thanked me. Then Doña Carlota and a whole bunch of other people I didn't know came to kiss me. The women had their eyes done like Cleopatra. And *caramba,* some of these ladies smelled good! Shalimar. Chanel No. 5. Those were perfumes Mami and I had tried at the stores but couldn't afford to buy. Most of these ladies, though, like Marisol's mother, had the fancy perfume smell mixed with the smell of cigarettes.

The two men who kissed me smoked too. The other men were busy playing dominoes. I saw their nails, so white, so clean, and so well trimmed that I wondered if they also went to the beauty parlor.

I was glad Papi and Mami hadn't come. Neither of them smoked. And Papi was right. He'd have had to clean his nails before he could come, and he couldn't have worn one of his shirts with *coquí* prints.

Mami thought she'd fit among these people, but she really didn't. Her nails were always clean, but she never used polish. Her blue chiffon dress would have been fine for this party, but she wouldn't fit in with her flats. These ladies wore spiky high-heeled shoes.

What would Mami and Papi wear for the carnival? That worried me, but then Katrina came. She hadn't said a word to me since she'd given me lice, and I hadn't congratulated her for being queen. But she kissed me. She'd started to say something when Marisol yanked my hand and took me to her bedroom.

A diary, a jewelry box, a stuffed dog, a necklace, and many other gifts covered Marisol's bed. She ripped open my gift. "Pretty! We can be twins!" This other dress Mami had made her was like the one I had on, except that the top fabric of one was the skirt of the other. "Did your mother make it?"

I nodded, though I'd have preferred to say that we bought it at Bonita Fashions.

When we came out, the other girls were talking by the door.

"Giraux," Katrina asked me, "you went to Cordero School, didn't you?"

"Yes," I said. "Why?"

"Do you know Ana Montañez?"

I didn't know if in moments like this the color could wash off from what Mami called an olive-white face, but I felt it did from mine. "Sh-she . . . she was in my class."

"Don't stutter. Just tell me if she's your friend."

I swallowed, looking at her blue polyester dress, the same one she'd worn for the contest. "No . . . she isn't my friend," I said, feeling disloyal to Ana one more time.

"But you know her, eh?" Like Abuelita's El Jacho, Katrina had many tongues of fire.

"I told you. She was in my class."

"Well, I want you to go to that school and talk to her. Tell her that she better get out of the carnival court, because a queen like me cannot have a princess like her." Katrina made a face. "My father says that people like her are bad, that they have no ambition. And they steal!"

Katrina didn't say it, but I knew she was talking about black people. I wasn't sure what her father meant by "no ambition." If he meant that blacks couldn't possibly be in "high society," well, they couldn't shed off their skin. But Ana had ambition! She went to school and had good grades. And Miss Bocachica was a teacher. And Cesar's father was a doctor!

Steal? Ana didn't steal. Neither did Miss Bocachica—nor Cesar. Not even Nora, who was so poor. Katrina and her father didn't know what they were talking about . . . but was that what high-society people thought of blacks? That they were thieves? That they were bad? That wasn't fair. I'd seen black thieves on the news, but I'd also seen white thieves.

I wanted to yell, "Ana isn't a thief!" But I couldn't defend her, because I'd said that we were not friends . . . and what if Marisol thought blacks were bad too? I didn't want to lose her friendship.

I stared at Katrina, wanting her to die like Tío Cansio, *de repente*. She couldn't hold my stare, so she studied me from head to toe. "Is that dress from Bonita Fashions?"

"Yes, it is!" Marisol said, and I felt like hugging her.

"Hmm!" Katrina moved her hand the way she used to when she wanted to toss back her long hair. But since she had short hair now, she tossed back the air instead. "I didn't think you could afford to buy a dress from Bonita Fashions."

"Well, as you can see, I can."

Katrina turned around and went downstairs, taking the other girls with her. Marisol and I stayed upstairs, our hands covering our mouths so Katrina couldn't hear us laughing.

"How come she gets to be queen? Ana . . . " I didn't want Marisol to know that Ana and I had been friends. I added her last name. "Montañez did better than Katrina. And . . . Ana Montañez needs the scholarship the queen gets. Katrina doesn't."

"I know, Tere, but Katrina really wants to be queen, and her father does anything for his darling daughter."

"He has something to do with this, eh?"

Marisol nodded. "A lot! See, he donates money to the city all the time, and he told the judges that if they didn't vote for Katrina, he wouldn't give one more penny."

"I'd be mad if somebody talked to me that way."

"Well, he didn't say it that way. I overheard my mother telling my father that he said it in a very convincing way." Marisol paused. "I don't remember the exact words—something about how he'd feel if they didn't choose Katrina to be queen, and something about the judges not appreciating everything he'd done for Ponce. But that, if by any chance Katrina won, he'd give thousands of dollars to build public housing for the people of San Antón."

"And take them out of their houses?" I said, alarmed.

Marisol shrugged. "I guess."

"But they like it the . . . " I caught myself in time. Nora liked living in San Antón, but I didn't want Marisol to know that I knew somebody who lived there. "Why do they want to move them out?" I asked.

"Don't ask me." Marisol began to walk downstairs.

I pulled her gently by her arm. "Did your mother vote for Katrina?"

"She did, and she feels really guilty about it."

"What about the mayor?" I said, following Marisol downstairs.

"He voted for Ana Montañez. . . . " Marisol lowered her voice. "My mother doesn't think Katrina's father dared tell the mayor what he told the other judges."

"It's not fair."

"I know," Marisol agreed.

When we made it down, Marisol took a basket with little pieces of folded paper. She asked every girl to take one for a raffle. "Okay," Marisol said, "open the papers." We did. "Who has number ten?"

Shyly, I held my paper up.

"You do?" Marisol asked with a big smile, giving me a beautiful sandalwood fan.

"You did that on purpose," Katrina complained.

A man, the only one wearing a suit and tie, came to her side. Katrina's father!

I held the fan tightly, remembering Papi's story about the ball he'd won at El Casino and how somebody had made him give it away.

Marisol's father stepped forward. "She didn't do it on purpose. Ten is the lucky number because today is Marisol's tenth birthday."

Katrina pinched her lips and gave me a hateful look. What she didn't get to know was that I got another treat.

We ate and sang "Happy Birthday to You" early because Marisol's grandparents had to go to San Juan. Marisol stood in front of the cake, her parents on one side, her four grandparents on the other, a professional photographer taking lots of pictures of them and the cake.

The cake had a maypole, though this was November, not May. At the center stood a frosting-covered pole from which came ten satin ribbons held by tiny dolls.

We sang the song we always sang after "Happy Birthday to You."

*"Feliz, feliz en tu día,*
"Happy, happy on your day,

*amiguita, que Dios te bendiga,*
God bless you, my friend,

*que reine la paz en tu día*
let peace reign on your day

*y que cumplas muchos más."*
and we wish you many more!"

Marisol blew out the candles, her family hugged her, then she gave each of us a doll from the cake. Mine was the only one wearing a tiny pearl necklace. And I felt special!

After Marisol's grandparents left, the orchestra began to play the limbo. Marisol pulled me into the line where everybody was dancing and going under the broom Marisol's parents were holding. They lowered it every time we went by. I knew how to dance limbo. Ana had taught me. Ana! I shook my head. No way Katrina would let her be princess.

My thoughts about Ana faded when Eva's and Katrina's mothers took off their spiky high-heeled shoes and joined us in the limbo. As they bent over backward to go underneath the broom, their beehives flapped, and I wondered if they had hairpieces. I wanted badly for one of them to lose her hairpiece.

But after one time through, they decided not to limbo anymore.

Marisol's parents kept lowering the broom. Olga and Eva and other people fell under it. They were out. Katrina, Marisol, and others who were cheating by going over the broom were out too. At the end it was just Katrina's father and me. He'd taken off his jacket and tie to dance the limbo. He danced it well, and I wondered where he'd learned it.

"Bravo!" people cheered when he went under the broom and made it through.

Marisol's parents lowered the broom—this time leaving almost no space between it and the floor. People clapped at the rhythm of the limbo music, and I danced until I got close. I bent my knees all the way to the ground. Slowly, I got myself under the broom. My belly almost touched it, but I squeezed my stomach in as tightly as I could and slipped my chest through, then my head. People applauded.

"Your turn!" they said to Katrina's father.

The underarms of his white long-sleeved shirt and his forehead were wet with sweat. But he bent his knees and squeezed himself under the broom. I thought his belly wouldn't make it, but it did. I rubbed my knees. They hurt. No way I could go one more time. But Katrina's father still had to get his head through. He could make it. Now he just had his forehead to go.

But then sweat dripped down from his forehead into his eye. He tried to wipe it off, and he fell!

Marisol's father helped him get up, then raised my hand. "The winner!" And people clapped.

"Congratulations," Katrina's father said to me, putting his jacket back on.

I thanked him, and then Marisol yanked me to line up again. This time even the orchestra got in line. We sang, "Ponce is Ponce!" kicking one leg to the side, then the other, dancing all over the house.

The orchestra switched to *"Paris se enciende; se enciende Paris,* Paris turns on its lights, it turns on its lights!" And we kept following the saxophone and trumpet players and dancing in line. I had so much fun that when the orchestra played and sang, *"Se acabó lo que se daba, se acabó. Se acabó lo que se daba, vamonos,* The party is over, let's go home," I felt like crying.

## 20

After Marisol's birthday Mami and I spent days washing our plastic sofa, hosing the stairs, painting over the telephone numbers written on the wall, and putting up the metallic Christmas tree Buela had bought for us. I liked the tree very much. It had a rotating color panel that made the tree look red now, then green, then yellow, then blue. In previous years we'd bought natural Christmas trees that came from the United States. I loved the smell of them, but way before January 6—*el día de los Reyes,* Three Kings' Day—they got dry and we had to throw them away. That wasn't going to happen this year.

Every night Mami stayed up really late sewing Christmas dresses for other people and cooking *pasteles* and *tembleque.* We had to be prepared, because during the Christmas season people came in *parrandas,* caroling at any time. Even late at night we got up, asked the carolers in, and fed them. But we also were getting ready for Marisol and her parents. Mami had invited them, and Papi couldn't understand why.

"They invited us to Marisol's birthday, and we didn't go," Mami tried to explain. "We have to reciprocate, Ramón."

I'd told Papi how wonderful Marisol's parents were with me, but he still didn't like them. He had no reason for not liking them. He'd only seen Doña Carlota briefly and had never met Marisol's father.

"To be frank with you, Dolores, I don't feel like being with *blanquitos*."

"Ramón!" Mami said angrily.

That made me upset too. *Blanquitos,* little whites, meant "stuck-up people," and I didn't want Papi to call Marisol that.

But the night of the party he came home early and went to take a shower.

As I started to comb my hair, I heard the doorbell, and I ran to open the door. It wasn't Marisol but one of Papi's customers.

I went to tell Papi. I thought he'd go out to tell the customer that he had a party, that he couldn't help him. But Papi went out to talk to him and came back to change into his coveralls.

"What are you doing?" Mami screamed. "We have guests coming."

"This man needs me to start his car," he said, putting on his work shoes. "And I'm not going to say no to him."

Mami was furious. And so was I. I wanted Papi to be clean when Marisol's father got here. I wanted him to have those nails clean.

But Papi left.

Still angry at him, I went to my bedroom to finish combing my hair. Although Papi had said I looked like an iguana, Mami let me comb it into a tight ponytail. Each day a few more hairs snapped, forming curly bangs. I tried to comb them down. They wouldn't cooperate.

It also bothered me that I didn't have a Christmas gift for Marisol. Mami wanted to wait until Three Kings' Day because things were cheaper after Christmas. But Marisol had already told me that she had a gift for me, and I wanted to have one for her.

While Mami was in the kitchen, I sneaked into her bedroom to peek in the jewelry box. I couldn't give Marisol my baby ring or the bracelet Mami had given me for my fifth birthday. I closed the jewelry box.

On the windowsill, I saw the miniature plastic sewing machine I'd given Mami for Mother's Day. I told myself I wasn't stealing. I thought stealing was the worst sin a child could commit. But Mami hadn't touched that sewing machine in ages.

I went to my bedroom, gift-wrapped the sewing machine, and hid it under my bed.

∽

When Marisol came with her mother and father, I kissed the three of them. Marisol was holding a gift wrapped in green metallic paper with a red velvet bow. I kept an eye on it while Mami kissed her. Then Papi rushed in.

"This . . . is Ramón," Mami said.

Marisol's father stretched out his hand, and Papi showed him his greasy hands. "Give me a few minutes to wash off and change."

"His customers have no consideration," Mami

said to Marisol's father after Papi was out of sight. "Anyway, come in, feel at home."

I snickered. How could they feel at home when their house was much better than ours?

I eyed Marisol's gift again. I wanted to go to my bedroom to open it and give her my gift. But Mami asked me to find the Perry Como Christmas record and play it. It took me a while. Papi had been playing records by Bobby Capó and Puerto Rican *décimas,* and he'd put the Perry Como at the bottom. When I finally found it, Papi came in. He smelled good. But he didn't look quite right wearing a green shirt with bright red poinsettias.

"Sorry," he told Marisol's parents.

"Don't worry," Marisol's father said. "I've been admiring your Jesus Smith." He pointed at the wall where we had the picture of the Sacred Heart of Jesus with blue eyes and red hair. "And your Jesús Rodríguez." He pointed at a side table where we displayed a picture of Jesus with dark brown eyes and dark hair.

It took me a few moments to get the joke. He was saying that the blue-eyed Jesus was American, the brown-eyed Jesús, a Puerto Rican. That didn't have to be true. Jeanette Simpson, an American, didn't have blue eyes. And Marisol—and Marisol's father himself—were Puerto Ricans who had red hair and aqua eyes.

Mami frowned. She found the joke disrespectful. But Papi laughed. Then Mami laughed too. I knew she'd laughed because she was glad to see Papi getting along with Marisol's father. So was I.

"Let's go to my bedroom." I took two peppermints from a dish on the center table, gave one to Marisol, dropped one in my mouth, and took Marisol with me.

She sat on my bed, the sleeve of her green-and-red taffeta dress touching my arm.

"Here!" She gave me the gift. "Open it!"

I carefully untied the ribbon, unwrapped the paper, and opened the box. "A two-piece swimsuit!" I twirled the bottom, then the top. Both pieces were yellow with white daisies. "Thank you. Thank you very much. I wanted one badly."

I rolled the peppermint in my mouth, bent down, and took Marisol's gift out from under the bed. "The wrapping paper isn't metallic like yours, but . . . here!"

Marisol ripped open the gift. "How cute!" She opened the sewing machine's tiny drawers. "Let me show it to my parents."

"No, no!" I gripped her skirt and stopped her from going out. "Don't tell anyone about the sewing machine. Okay, Marisol? I . . . I always wanted to have a special secret with my best friend, and I want this one to be ours."

Marisol looked puzzled, but said, "Okay, okay. I won't show it to anybody."

She put it in her black patent-leather purse, and I sighed.

"Do you hear a guitar?" I asked her, tilting my

head toward the window to listen. *Shaka-shaka-shaka.* "Maracas! *A parranda!*"

Marisol and I ran out, and I opened the door before Mami, who was turning off the record player, or Papi could get it.

Ana's parents—and Ana! I felt like slamming the door and blocking it with my body so nobody could open it. But Papi said behind me, "Come in, come in."

They stepped forward, Don Toño playing the guitar and Doña Monse the maracas. Ana stood by the Christmas tree, singing with her parents. "*Hermoso bouquet, aquí te traemos bellísimas flores del jardín riqueño,* Beautiful bouquet, we have come to bring you these lovely flowers from the Puerto Rican garden." Her lips had no smile. She looked at Marisol, then at me.

I felt embarrassed because I'd been mean to Ana, and here she was wishing me a Merry Christmas. I also felt embarrassed because Ana was dressed like a *jíbara,* a Puerto Rican peasant, wearing a white blouse embroidered with a pig being roasted on a spit, the ruffled red-and-green skirt she'd worn for the pageant, a bunch of bean necklaces and round bracelets, and no shoes! She also had her hair loose—frizzy and bushy. But my biggest worry was that Marisol could get to know that I'd lied—that Ana Montañez really had been my friend.

I stood by Marisol, hoping my body could hide Ana. Marisol was taller. She could see Ana over me if she wanted. I looked around to see what everybody else was doing. Papi was singing. Mami? Her lips were tight, her eyes looking from me to Ana. Marisol's father was sitting comfortably on our awful sofa, tapping his foot to the rhythm of the music. Doña Carlota? Singing and clapping, cigarette in hand.

I hoped Marisol's parents were thinking that Ana and her parents were strangers. But most people went on *parrandas* to visit friends.

When the song ended, Papi introduced them. They all shook hands except Ana, who stayed by our Christmas tree watching it change colors.

"Sit, sit," Papi insisted.

I didn't want them to sit.

"Yes," Mami said, her face red as if she was embarrassed. "Come and eat a little . . . something."

*"No, gracias,"* Don Toño said. "We want to go to other friends' houses. Would you like to join us?"

Somehow I could tell that Ana hadn't told her parents everything I'd done to her.

"We can't go this year," Mami answered with a sad voice.

"That's all right." Doña Monse peeked at Marisol's parents over Mami's shoulder and nodded. "We understand."

For a moment I also felt sad, remembering how much fun I'd had the year before. Ana's parents came with a *parranda,* and we joined them. We stayed awake all night, going from house to house, then had breakfast at Ana's house.

"Don't let us stop you, Dolores," Doña Carlota said.

"¡Ay, no! You're not stopping us. We were planning to stay here tonight and that's what we're doing." Mami looked at Don Toño. "Another time."

Doña Monse and Don Toño shook hands with everybody again and waved, saying, "¡Feliz Navidad!"

When they left, Papi said, "Ana was Teresa's best friend at Cordero School."

I wished Papi hadn't said that.

"Ah!" Doña Carlota snapped her fingers. "Now I know who she is. How could I forget? She's the carnival princess."

"They seem like very nice people," Marisol's father said.

Mami nodded. "They're *morenos*, but they're good people."

Mami was talking like Katrina, hinting that most blacks were bad.

Papi frowned and opened his mouth to say something, but Mami jumped in. "Let's eat."

I couldn't get out of it so quickly. Though I tried to move with everybody else to the dining room, Marisol held me back. "Ana Montañez, the carnival princess, is your best friend?"

"Not anymore."

"Why not?"

"Because you're my best friend now," I said, walking toward the dining room.

"You can have two best friends."

"That's true, but the two of you would have to be friends, and would your parents let you have a black friend?" I was testing Marisol. I wanted to know what she and her parents thought about her being friends with black people.

Marisol shrugged. "My parents won't mind. They want me to be friends with all kinds of people."

It would have been neat to have my two best friends be friends. But Ana wasn't my friend anymore. And even if she was, she'd never be able to go to El Escorial with us. Katrina and her father wouldn't allow it.

༄

Later on, when Marisol and her parents were gone and I was carrying the dishes to the kitchen, Papi called, "Teresa, there is a gift under the Christmas tree for you."

I rushed to the living room, hoping Marisol had left another gift. It wasn't from Marisol. A small card said:

Teresa (Not Tere),

*Yo tengo la otra mitad del corazón,*
I have the other half of the heart.

*Y dice: "Best."*
And it says, "Best."

I unwrapped the Christmas paper, and opened the velvet box that had a charm, a half heart that said "Friends." It wasn't on a bracelet like the one I wanted to give Marisol, but on a chain.

Ana's note said that she had the other half of the heart. If the two halves were put together, the heart would say "Best Friends." I could see the two of us, sitting in the shade of the *níspero* tree, putting the heart together.

"That's very nice, Teresa." Papi sounded sad.

I looked at the charm again. Now all I saw was a broken heart. A broken friendship. And, for a moment, I felt sorry I'd broken it.

"What is it?"

I showed Mami the chain. "A gift from Ana."

I thought she'd say, "Ah, but this isn't real gold." Instead, she burst into tears.

"Why are you crying?" I asked.

Mami shook her head and went to wash dishes. I didn't understand what was going on with her. It was weird!

೭ఌ

As soon as I got up the next day, I took the chain out of its box. Pretty! I didn't think about El Escorial and its carnival but about Ana and the good times we'd had together: playing passport and tag, spinning the hibiscus flowers, planning the marshmallow wedding, celebrating Miss Bocachica's marriage—sharing our secrets in the shade of the *níspero* tree.

Maybe Ana was ready to be my friend again. Maybe if I called her and thanked her . . .

I went to the hallway to phone Ana. "*Hola,*" I said when she answered.

"Who is this?"

"Tere . . . "

"What do you want?"

I looked at the charm in my hand. "I want to thank you for the pretty chain."

"Don't thank me," Ana answered. "Thank Miss Bocachica, who wrote asking me to be your friend again. Thank my parents, who bought the chain even though they couldn't afford it." Silence. Then, "Don't thank me. Thank them! They made me do it."

I clenched my teeth. Who was Ana to speak to me like that? "Well," I said, "my parents made me call you too. So there!"

Another lie! Ana had made me lie again! I slammed the phone, went crying to my bedroom, threw the chain on my bed, and took a shoe to break it into pieces. I hit the mattress; I hit my pillow; I even hit my hand. But I didn't hit the chain. I couldn't, and I didn't know why.

## 21

Santa Claus brought me clothes every year. But on January 5, I always left grass and water under my bed for the camels of the Three Kings to eat and drink. The next morning instead of grass I would find the toys I'd wanted. That year I'd asked for a Minnie Mouse watch. I got color pencils instead.

"The Three Kings are poor this year," Mami said when she saw my disappointment.

I felt like throwing the pencils in the waste basket and screaming, "This is not what I wanted!" Then I remembered that I'd made Mami buy a bracelet to give Marisol on Three Kings' Day. Also, we had to save money for the carnival.

Mami could make my gown, but the sequins and beads were expensive. The headpiece Mrs. Pérez had ordered cost twenty-five dollars. "We can't afford that much—unless we don't drink milk for months," Mami had said.

That same week when I'd showed her that we were running out of toothpaste, she'd cut open the tube and made me use the little bit of toothpaste attached to the inside. So I knew how tight money was. But I also knew that I would be the joke of the class if I was the only one not going to the carnival. Besides, I wanted a gown badly.

Marisol's gown turned out very pretty. The skirt's green-velvet pleats opened to a layer of creamy-colored tulle. Mami told Marisol the tulle was the inside of the *guanábana;* black beads would be the seeds.

I prayed to God to please let Mami have enough money to make me a gown like that.

One night while Mami sewed beads onto Marisol's gown, I asked her, "What about me? What about my gown?"

"You're going to be a *níspero.*"

"A *níspero?*"

"It's your favorite fruit, isn't it?"

"Not anymore."

Mami left the room. I didn't see any reason for her to be angry or disappointed, but I saw some of that in her frown. Mami *had* to understand. Nobody ate *nísperos* at La Academia. It was a poor person's fruit . . . brown . . . rough.

Mami stood by the door, holding a beautiful golden-brown gown. In places leaves decorated with sequins gathered up the skirt. The bottom of the gown had a layer of golden-brown tulle topped by creamy-colored tulle. The creamy layer made the golden brown look lighter. Like the inside of a . . . *níspero.*

"I'd planned to glue on beads for the seeds, but you don't want to be a *níspero.*"

All I could say was, "How could you pay for all that tulle?"

"I didn't. The creamy tulle is a leftover piece from Marisol's gown, and I took the golden tulle from the dress you wore to Miss Bocachica's wedding."

"I loved that dress."

Mami placed her hand on my shoulder. "Did you really love it?" Her voice sounded sad.

"Yes," I said, noticing the row of little buttons on the back of the *níspero* gown. "But I love this one more. Much more! Can I try it on? Please, please."

She let me put it on. I couldn't believe it. The gown was even prettier than Marisol's. "I look like a queen!" I saw myself in the mirror. "Like a *real* queen!" I twirled around, the skirt moving from side to side. I waltzed all over the house, Mami behind me, telling me to be careful, not to get it caught on anything, not to get it dirty. Then she showed me a gown with turquoise sequins.

"For Marisol's mother?" I asked.

"No, for me."

My mouth fell open.

"You didn't think I'd embarrass you by wearing the dress I wore to Miss Bocachica's wedding, did you?"

I'd been worried about that, but I said, "I didn't think you had the money or the time to make yourself a new dress."

"Teresa, I'll do anything for my daughter." Mami

put her arm around my shoulder. "I even reserved a tuxedo for your Papi. All we have to do now is wait for the membership letter from El Escorial."

～

Five days later the letter came. "Mami! Mami! It's here!"

I sat next to Mami as she ripped open the envelope. She read, "'We regret we cannot accept your application to El Club Escorial de Ponce.'" Mami didn't bother reading the rest. It was signed by Rogelio Colón, President. Katrina's father.

I cried, "Katrina and her father want to stomp us like roaches!"

"*Ajá.*" Mami nodded. "And her mother thinks you're too *trigueñita,* dark for them."

I thought maybe I should try the lemon juice one more time.

"We're also too poor for them," Mami added.

"Could you sew more dresses? Could you do something to make more money?"

But I knew she couldn't.

"Don't tell Papi," Mami said.

"Don't tell me what?" Papi said, suddenly appearing in the doorway.

Mami lowered her eyes and gave Papi the envelope. She cried, "I even made myself a gown for the carnival and ordered you a tuxedo. All for nothing. How stupid of me. How stupid!"

Papi read the letter, then threw it on the table. "Maybe I should move out and let the two of you make the decisions in this house."

I clutched Papi by his waist. "No, Papi, no. I love you."

"Well, maybe you and your mother should listen to me once in a while."

"We will, Ramón. We will."

～

That night I heard Mami crying. "I have been blind, Ramón. I thought La Academia people were better than the Cordero people, but I was wrong!"

Silence. I got out of bed, trying to hear better. I thought I'd hear Papi, but he didn't say anything. He probably was still feeling angry and hurt.

He just let Mami talk. "Katrina's parents have humiliated us over and over. Ramón, you have no idea of what I've gone through."

Mami told Papi about the call she got from Katrina's mother when I got lice, about her calling me *trigueñita* and saying not to send me to school until my head was clear. I expected Papi to say, "Well, those are things you did to Ana and her parents." But Mami said it.

"*Ay,* Ramón, I need to apologize to Monse and Toño." Mami sniffled. "I'll never forget their happy faces when they came singing on Christmas. But I was ashamed of them, Ramón." Mami was sobbing now. "I even told Teresa that she couldn't bring Ana home if Marisol and Doña Carlota were here. But what if somebody did that to Teresa? How would I feel?" Mami paused. "What am I saying? Some parents from La Academia are probably doing this to Teresa already. *Ay,* Ramón, I deserve this."

*Caramba,* I'd never thought about that. Katrina, Olga, and Eva had never invited me to their houses. They probably had had birthday parties, and they didn't invite me.

But I didn't care that much. What was *really* important to me now was that Marisol continued to be my friend, that I could go to El Escorial and to school with her, and that I could wear my gown to the carnival.

∽

On the night of the carnival dress rehearsal Papi drove me to the gate of El Escorial. I got out of the car, and Mami handed me the gown in a box. Mrs. Pérez had asked us to change at El Escorial so no outsiders could see our dresses until the carnival.

"We'll wait for you in the car," Mami said.

I kissed them. "May God bless you," Papi said.

I walked through the gate, where a guard stopped me. I told him that I was an Academia girl, but he didn't let me in until he'd called the main office and cleared my name with them.

The pool's dressing rooms were not only loud, they also had stuff scattered all over. Shirts on the floor. Bobby pins on the sinks. Katrina's Minnie Mouse watch sat beside her on a bench. I passed Katrina. Her brocade pineapple gown looked beautiful, but mine was prettier!

The maid, picking up after the girls, said that soon she'd leave to watch the dress rehearsal. I passed Eva and Olga. Pretty gowns! I waved at Marisol, who also looked beautiful in her *guanábana* gown, and stepping over clothes, I went to Mrs. Pérez.

"I'm sorry I'm late."

"Much too late to change. Here, just wear your headpiece." She gave me the papier-mâché *níspero* tree. "Before you go home, return it to this box. And do the same the night of the carnival. I want to display them at school."

I was putting on the headpiece when Marisol yelled, "Stop it!"

I turned and saw Katrina trying to open *my* box. Marisol pushed her away.

"Girls, girls," Mrs. Pérez said. "Come on, come on, line up."

We lined up and walked to the dancing-hall entrance, where we had to wait a long time for other groups to rehearse. Boring. I couldn't see the people rehearsing, and my neck hurt because I had to hold my head up so that the papier-mâché tree wouldn't fall.

Marisol got out of the line to talk to me. "Tere," she whispered, her hand holding in place the *guanábana* tree on her head. "The mayor knows what Katrina's father did and about Katrina saying that Ana couldn't be princess, and he told Katrina that she cannot be queen."

I put my hand on Marisol's arm. "Who is the queen then?"

"Ana!"

I squeezed Marisol's arm. Then I opened my eyes wide. "Who told the mayor? Your mother?"

Marisol shushed me, and I said really loud, "Katrina must be furious!"

Katrina heard me. "I'm not furious. People think the mayor told me that I couldn't be queen, but *I* told him!"

Out of the corner of my eye I saw Marisol shaking her head. Katrina was lying.

"Ha! That friend of yours, Giraux, doesn't even have a gown. All she has is a stupid crepe-paper dress."

I knew exactly the dress Katrina was talking about. Doña Monse had made it the year before for Ana to be a violet at a school play. It wasn't a dress for a queen.

Katrina stared at me with a pinched, mean face. "If she wears that dress, she's going to be the laugh of Ponce!"

I felt my anger growing, overflowing. How dare this mean daughter of snobs pick on Ana!

"It's true what my father says." Katrina shrugged. "Who wants to be remembered as the white queen with a black princess?"

I looked Katrina straight in her eyes. "You know what, Katrina Kolón Katalán? You're spoiled rotten!"

The other girls gasped.

Katrina didn't have a tree on her head because pineapples don't grow on trees. She had a pineapple instead, its sharp leaves looking as dangerous as her piercing eyes. "I am not!"

"You are! And because of that, you are nothing. Nothing!"

Before she could grab my headpiece and hair, I turned around and ran to the dressing room. Inside, I threw my headpiece in Mrs. Pérez's box and picked up my gown. On the way out I saw Katrina's Minnie Mouse watch. And I took it.

# 22

When I came out of El Escorial, Mami and Papi were waiting in the car, Mami with her head on Papi's chest, sleeping. As soon as Papi saw me, he woke her up.

"How was it?" Mami asked when I closed the car door.

I shrugged. "All right."

"Whose watch is that?" Papi said, looking back. Mami also looked.

"Katrina's. She lent it to me . . . until after the carnival." I said it remembering that, because of the rehearsals, La Academia didn't have classes for a whole week.

Papi and Mami glanced at each other, puzzled.

I couldn't sleep that night, wondering if anybody had seen me stealing the watch. I also wondered what had happened to me. I'd turned bad, as bad as a rotten pineapple. That thought made me laugh—a nervous laugh—because Katrina was representing a pineapple, and I'd turned as bad as she. Spoiled rotten. Worse yet, I was a thief! I didn't want to be that way. I didn't!

The next morning, before Sunday Mass, I went to confession so I could feel better and take Communion. First I told Padre Mario that I'd lied. "What else?" he asked.

"I haven't been good to my friends." This I also told him every time I'd confessed, after leaving Cordero.

"What else?" Padre Mario said again.

"I . . . I stole a Minnie Mouse watch."

I thought he'd give me a long speech, but he asked, "Do you still have it?"

"Yes."

"Anything else?"

"No . . . nothing else."

"Pray ten Our Fathers and ten Hail Marys . . . and return that watch."

I'd planned to do that, to put the watch where Katrina could find it.

I returned to the pew, knelt, closed my eyes tight, and prayed the ten Our Fathers and ten Hail Marys. It didn't help. I still felt full of sin. I didn't take Communion.

When we got home, Don Felipe crossed the street to talk to us. But I heard our phone ringing, so I grabbed Papi's house keys, ran upstairs, and answered it.

"Have you seen my watch?" Marisol asked.

I didn't answer, and Marisol continued. "Katrina

says she saw you . . . taking it. I don't believe her, but I can't find it."

My mouth trembled. I had not stolen *Katrina's* watch. I'd stolen Marisol's.

I hung up and burst into tears.

"What happened?" Mami asked when she and Papi came in.

"I stole Marisol's watch!"

Mami put her hands on my shoulders. "But you said Katrina lent it to you."

"I lied. I stole Marisol's watch thinking it was Katrina's."

"But why?" Mami asked.

"Because I wanted to have a Minnie Mouse watch . . . and because Katrina is mean."

I could already see Katrina telling everybody that I'd stolen Marisol's watch. At the same time, I deserved that. I was worse than Katrina. I was a thief!

"I want to go back to Cordero," I said, sobbing.

Papi gave me his handkerchief, took out his comb, and sat me on the sofa by him. "Teresa, you . . . " He cleared his throat, combing his hair. "You can't change schools every time you have a problem."

I hit the sofa with my heel. "Don't worry. I can't go back to Cordero."

"Why?" Mami asked.

Like a faucet that hadn't been opened for a long time, my thoughts and words started rushing out, muddy, rusty, but then becoming clearer and clearer.

I told them why I'd left Cordero and how mean I'd been to Ana. "I am a liar! I am a fake! I am greedy! I am a thief!" Papi shushed me, but I continued. "I thought I was better than Ana, but she's better than me. Much better!"

"¡Ay!" Mami cried. "This is all my fault."

"No, Mami, no, it isn't all your fault. I've done a lot of bad things you don't know about. I even took your little sewing machine and gave it to Marisol for Christmas."

Mami covered her mouth.

"I'm sorry, Mami. I'm sorry."

Mami began to cry too. "It's my fault! I'm the one who said you couldn't be Ana's friend."

"Mami, you never told me I couldn't be friends with Ana."

"Maybe not, but I made you hide Ana's friendship from Abuelita, and I really wanted you to stop being her friend. So you did." She threw her hands up. "And look what happened!"

Papi went to Mami and took her in his arms. "Dolores, this isn't the end of the world. We can change this."

Mami rested her forehead on Papi's chest. "¡Ay, Ramón! I've turned our nice daughter into a thief!"

"I can return the watch," I said.

Papi glanced at me. "We know you will." Then he took Mami's chin and made her look at him.

"I know this can be fixed," she said, touching the collar of his *coquí* shirt. "But it won't be all that easy for me, Ramón. I'm even scared to tell my mother that Teresa and Ana are friends."

Papi shrugged. "Why?"

"That will kill her!"

I closed my eyes. I didn't want anything to kill Abuelita.

Papi laughed. "She might not like it, but it won't kill her."

"You don't think so?" Mami asked.

"I *know* it won't."

Papi sat Mami on the sofa, then sat between us. She leaned her head on his shoulder, and he rested his head on hers. They stayed like that for a few minutes.

It felt quiet. Peaceful.

Papi kissed Mami's forehead. "You know what we need?" he said in a whisper as if not to disturb the silence.

"What?" Mami asked, whispering too.

"To work less and spend more time together."

He touched my head with his head. "And be more with this precious girl."

Precious? I didn't feel precious.

I stood up. "I have to return the watch and I want to go talk to Ana. Could you take me?"

"Okay," Papi said.

I took a couple of steps to go, then, remembering that I'd never talked to my parents about Ana's coronation, I turned around. "Do you know that Ana is the carnival queen?"

Papi nodded. "Don Felipe just told us."

"That's great!" Mami said. "Ana deserves it."

"But she doesn't have a gown, and she can't go wearing . . . Mami! Could we give my gown to Ana?"

"Ha!" That was Papi.

Mami said, "I suppose you can go to the carnival at El Escorial on Saturday, then give the gown to Ana for her to wear on Sunday. That is, if Ana is still your size."

"No, Mami, I don't want to go to the carnival at El Escorial, and I don't want to wear the gown at all . . . " I stopped, worried that I'd hurt Mami's feelings. "I do like the gown, Mami. I like it a lot! But I want the gown to be Ana's. Just Ana's!"

Mami nodded, smiling. "You're right. It should be just hers."

"Great! All right!" Papi stood up and hugged me. He drew Mami into the hug and added, "After Marisol's house, we'll take the gown to Queen Ana!"

❧

On the way to Marisol's house my mouth trembled. The ride felt too short and way too soon we were knocking at her door.

Marisol opened it, and Doña Carlota, standing behind her, said, "Come in."

As we stepped into the family room, I gave Marisol her watch.

"Where did you find it?" she asked, bouncing with happiness.

"I . . . stole it last night. I thought it was Katrina's."

Doña Carlota's mouth fell open, and I moved closer to Papi and Mami.

Papi said, "It doesn't matter whose watch it is, does it, Teresa?"

I shook my head and buried my face in his shirt, crying.

Doña Carlota patted my shoulder. "You did the right thing by returning it, Teresa."

"She's very sorry, Marisol," Mami said. "Aren't you, Teresa?"

Papi tried to push me away from him. I clutched tighter, nodding so Marisol and her mother could tell I was sorry.

I was acting like a baby, but I was embarrassed, so embarrassed that I didn't dare look at Marisol. Finally, when we were leaving, I glanced at her. She didn't smile, and she didn't come to the car like she usually did.

"Marisol is never going to trust me again," I told my parents as soon as Papi began to drive down the hill.

"I think she will," Mami said. "But it may take time."

"You'll have to earn back her trust." Papi looked at me in the mirror. "You have to prove that you won't steal again. You can do that, can't you?"

"*Ajá,* I can do that."

On our way to Ana's, I decided I'd tell Marisol everything, as I'd told Papi and Mami. I knew she'd understand.

∽

When we got to Ana's house, Mami asked me, "Do you want us to go up with you?"

Papi interrupted. "No, Dolores. You already apologized to Toño and Monse. Now it's Teresa's turn. Like you, she has to do it alone."

I didn't know Mami had talked to Ana's parents. That would make it easier for me, I thought. Ana now would be more open to forgive me.

I got out of the car, climbed the few stairs to Ana's porch and knocked on the door. I could tell that Ana was alone because she opened her bedroom window a tiny bit and peeked out. I saw her *níspero* eyes peering at me. I waved, and she immediately closed the window. I waited, but she didn't open the door.

I knocked twice. I waited, then knocked again. "Ana! It's Teresa."

She didn't open. I knocked harder. "Ana, I know you're there. Open, please. I need to talk to you."

Nothing.

I could tell that my parents had seen everything, because when I went back to the car, Mami said, "Ramón, Teresa needs our help."

"No, we can't interfere," Papi insisted. "Teresa, what do you think you can do next?"

I thought for a few moments. "I can try calling her."

"Okay, let's go home, and you can call her."

When we were leaving, I glanced back and saw Ana peeking out the window. I thought she was probably regretting not opening the door. So as soon as we got home, I phoned her.

"Ana . . ."

"Teresa Giraux, we don't have anything to talk about." Then, *clunk!*

"She hung up on me!" I cried to my parents.

"Teresa, you don't have school tomorrow, but Ana does," Mami said, caressing my curls. "You can go to Cordero in the morning and give it another try." She turned to Papi. "If that doesn't work, please, Ramón, let's help her. Let's take her to Ana's house in the evening and try together."

"Okay," Papi said. "But, Teresa, you need to understand how Ana feels. You've hurt her a lot. It may take time for her to trust you too."

"I know, Papi."

౿

The next morning I picked up the box with the gown and went to Cordero.

Everything looked the same, the *trinitaria* vines, the hibiscus flowers, the *níspero* tree.

"Hey, look who's here," Cesar said when he saw me.

Ana, who was running, slowed to a walk, then stopped. She stuck her fists on her hips. "Why are you following me around? I told you—we don't have anything to talk about."

Linda came and studied me—from head to toe. "You look different. Prettier."

I didn't know why she said that. I had my hair down and had on the dress I wore to Marisol's birthday—now too worn to wear to La Academia girls' parties.

"Are you coming back to Cordero?" Cesar asked.

"In August . . . if Miss Bocachica comes back." Papi had decided I should finish the year at La Academia. Next year he wanted me to go to Cordero. He'd heard that Mrs. Ortega wasn't getting along with my class, and that Miss Bocachica might come back because of that and because her husband had to serve outside of the United States.

"*Ajá.*" Cesar nodded. "Miss Bocachica is coming back."

I smiled and turned to Ana. "Please, let me talk to you . . . alone."

"These are my friends," she said. "If you have something to say, say it to all of us."

I took a deep breath. "I lied to you. . . . " I swallowed to keep my tears in. "And I know I've been mean to you. So I came to say I'm sorry."

"*¡Ajá!* " Linda said. "Now that she's queen, you come to say you're sorry."

Ana folded her arms and waited for me to say something.

"That's not why I'm saying it. . . . " I put my hand on my chest and felt the charm Ana had given me. I pulled it out from under my dress.

Ana touched her charm, then took her hand away. "I saw you one day on the street. I know you saw me, but you ran away."

She must have told this to Linda and Cesar, because they nodded.

"I know . . . I don't know why I ran away. . . . I

guess I was being stuck up. But I'm not like that. . . . Not anymore."

Ana looked down and flattened a chunk of dry mud with her loafer.

"Ana, I want to be your friend again . . . and yours, Linda, and yours, Cesar."

"You have another friend," Ana said. "You don't need us."

"You mean Marisol? She's nice. I'd like you to meet her."

Ana shrugged and pulled Linda by her arm. "Let's play tag."

They headed toward the *níspero* tree, Cesar following them.

"I brought you this!" I yelled.

All three of them stopped and turned.

I walked slowly toward Ana and gave her the box. She set it on top of the hibiscus hedge, opened it, and took out the gown.

*"¡Mama mía!"* Linda said.

Ana threw the gown back in. "I already have a dress for the carnival."

"You do." Linda took the gown back out. "But it's not as pretty as this."

Ana made Linda put the gown back in. "I know what she is trying to do. She's giving me a gown that her friend Katrina has seen, so Katrina can have a good laugh."

"Katrina is *not* my friend."

Ana waved me off. She didn't believe me.

I stayed quiet for a moment, trying to find a way to prove that I was saying the truth. "Katrina gave me lice."

Linda came closer. "She did?"

Ana squinted, peering at me. "Are you lying again? I don't think La Academia girls can get lice."

"They do! I got them from Katrina. But she blamed hers on me, and Katrina's mother called Mami to tell her not to send me to school until I had no head lice."

Ana nodded, probably remembering when Mami kept me home because Ana had lice.

"Katrina calls me Giraux. She hates me that much."

"She hates me too," Ana whispered.

"Ana, believe me." I almost touched her arm, but afraid she wouldn't allow it, I didn't. "Katrina hasn't seen the gown. Nobody has seen it but Mami and me and now you. It was my gown, but I'm not going to the carnival at El Escorial. I have many reasons for not wanting to go—but it's mostly because I want to give my gown to you."

Cesar stepped forward. "Why?"

"Because I want Ana to be the most beautiful junior queen . . . " I bit my lip to keep my tears from coming out. They came out anyway. I swallowed. "Please, Ana, take the gown."

Ana stared at me for a moment. She placed her hand on her charm. Linda and Cesar waited for her to say something. Slowly, Ana nodded. "Okay, Tere. When I get home, I'll try on the gown."

*"¡Chévere!"* Linda said.

I felt like hugging Ana, but instead I turned around and skipped all the way home. Ana had called me Tere again.

# 23

*T*he night of the Ponce carnival, the sky wore a black velvet gown with rhinestones. At first I thought the crescent moon was its crown, then I changed my mind. It had to be a smile—a happy smile, like mine.

Earlier that day Papi and I had gone to Coamo to get my grandparents. On the way there, Papi told me that even if I went to Cordero, Mami could keep on sewing a little bit and designing dresses for people so we could have an easier life. "Then you can buy gifts for your friends and things that you like to have for yourself. And your mother can go to the beauty parlor once in a while, and maybe I can even buy a *guayabera* or two."

"Did Mami like the idea?" I asked him.

Papi nodded. "She loves to design clothes, and I can see why. She's very good at it!" Papi opened his eyes wide. "If she gets famous, maybe I can take some college courses."

I giggled. I'd suspected all along that Papi still wanted to go to college, and I had the feeling that Mami would like it if he did.

Mami hadn't gone with us to Coamo because she had to do errands with Doña Carlota. I couldn't imagine what kinds of errands because, after all, the El Escorial carnival was over. But I knew that when Mami said, "I have to do errands," she meant grown-up stuff.

On the way back from Coamo Papi broke the big news to Buela, Buelo, and Abuelita. "Do you know that Ana Montañez, the carnival queen, has been Teresa's best friend since kindergarten?"

"Really?" Buelo said, looking at me from the front seat. "That's great! You should feel proud."

I knew I was supposed to answer, but my eyes were on Abuelita. I didn't want her to die.

She pinched her lips with her toothless gums, then said, "I saw that girl in the newspaper. She's black."

"Black, white, green—who cares!" Buela said. "She deserves to be queen. She's certainly nicer than that Colón Catalán girl."

"How come I didn't know of this friendship?" Abuelita asked me.

I shrugged. "I think Mami was afraid to tell you."

"Does she approve?"

"Kind of."

There was silence, a silence in which Abuelita kept pinching her lips with her gums, and Papi kept watching her in the mirror.

Finally, Abuelita shrugged. "Well, that's *your* problem. After all, Teresa is *your* daughter."

I sighed. Abuelita didn't die. What a relief!

❧

By the time we got back to Ponce, Mami was home waiting for us. I could tell that Abuelita wanted to talk to Mami, but we gave her no time. We walked together to La Plaza Las Delicias—Papi, Buelo, and I each carrying two wooden folding chairs. The extra one I carried was for Abuelita.

We set the chairs by the curb in front of El Parque de Bombas, the old firehouse, and sat. Playing with Abuelita's flappy arms, I watched as people filled up the sidewalks. Abuelita didn't talk, and I wondered if she was thinking about my friendship with Ana.

Then I heard Mami call. "Carlota! Here!"

I stood up, looked behind me, and saw Marisol stretching out her arm so I could grab it, and she could get to me. I took her hand, and she walked past her parents, Mami, Papi, Buelo, and Buela, who were now standing up. Papi and Marisol's father embraced in a hug. Papi didn't think that Marisol's parents were stuck up anymore. Still, Papi's hug surprised me.

I had my hair down, and Marisol touched my curls. "I love your hair that way."

I thanked her. Then, seeing Abuelita watching Marisol with curiosity, I said, "This is Marisol, Abuelita."

Abuelita gave her a toothless smile, and Marisol gave her one full of braces.

Marisol and I sat on the curb, and she whispered to me, "I want you to know that you didn't steal my watch."

I lowered my eyes, ashamed once more of what I'd done. Then, realizing what Marisol had just said, I perked up.

Marisol nodded. "You stole Katrina's watch. When she couldn't find it in the mess, the maid came in with my watch, and Katrina took it."

My mouth fell open. Marisol kept going. "I knew something was wrong, because my watch didn't have an extra hole on its band, and the watch you gave me did. I called Katrina today and told her that I knew what she'd done. She's saying now that Ponce is too small a town for her, that she and her family are moving to San Juan."

"*¡Ay!*" I said. "Poor girls of San Juan!"

We laughed.

The police motorcycles were coming, so we began to watch the parade. They formed circles, rows, and squares, and roared loudly.

Behind them came Uvita, a man who always walked in parades dressed like a soldier; then the Fire Department band played and, behind it, one of their old fire engines rang a bell. Then came a float with the San Juan queen dressed in a turquoise butterfly outfit, her wings moving back and forth. So pretty! We clapped, and threw confetti at her. Behind her came a *comparsa*—a costumed group of Cuban dancers wearing shirts with ruffles, the women with fruit baskets on their heads. They were playing, dancing, and singing, "*Al carnaval de Oriente me voy . . .* to the Orient carnival I go . . . "

After they left, there was a gap in the parade. I could see *vejigantes*, people dressed in colorful bat-like costumes and masks with pointy horns. But they were far away. I stretched out my legs and rested my head on Abuelita's leg. Marisol stood up and looked behind us, where our parents were, among the crowd. "Look! Eva and her mother!"

I stood up. "Eva!" I don't know why I was happy to see her—probably because I was just happy.

"We were at the beginning of the parade," Eva's mother said as soon as she finished kissing Doña Carlota. "And we saw the junior queen. Her gown is gorgeous! It must have cost a fortune, but I still want to know who the designer is."

Doña Carlota pointed at Mami. "Dolores is the designer!"

My smile got big. Ana was wearing my gown!

"Are you Dolores?" Eva's mother asked.

"She's Teresa's mother," Doña Carlota said, making me feel proud.

"And you made Marisol's gown too!" Eva's mother said. "You're a genius! Next year I want *you* to design Eva's gown."

Marisol elbowed me. Then she took Eva's hand and got her to join us by the curb.

"This is Eva, Abuelita."

Eva frowned at Abuelita's smile, and I shrugged. It was Eva's problem if she didn't like my grandmother's toothless smile. Then Mami surprised me, bringing my friends' parents to meet Abuelita! That made me even more proud of Mami.

The *vejigantes* were coming! As soon as they got closer, I moved to the street, calling Marisol and Eva to follow me. I walked behind the *vejigantes* and teased them:

"*Vejigante comió mangó*
"*Vejigante* ate mango,

*Y hasta las uñas se las lamió.*"
And he even licked his nails."

A *vejigante,* wearing a mask with at least seven horns, turned around and shook a *vejiga,* an inflated cow bladder full of dry beans. I ran away from him, laughing.

As soon as he turned his back to me, I went behind him and pulled one of the jingle bells on his bright red-and-yellow costume. Eva and Marisol did too. He chased us to the curb and walked away.

We held hands and moved closer and closer to him. When he turned around, we screamed and ran away. This time he threw a bunch of pennies at us and ran to join the other *vejigantes.*

"That was fun!" Eva said, picking up pennies.

Then I saw Cesar and Linda sitting on a convertible. He was the junior prince, she, the princess . . . wearing Marisol's gown!

Marisol shrugged when I looked at her. "My father told me . . . " She glanced at Eva, who was watching the parade. Marisol whispered the rest, "That you gave your gown to Ana, and I told him that I wanted to do that too."

That explained why Papi had hugged Marisol's father. Then I remembered Mami's errands. "*¡Ajá!* So that's what Mami and your mother were doing this morning?"

Marisol nodded. "We went to Linda's house. Your mother had to sew a lot for my gown to fit Linda."

As the car passed by us, Linda and Cesar waved at me. Linda saw Marisol and waved harder. "*¡Gracias!*"

The band from the School of Music followed Linda's car. All the players, including Nora, who was playing the maracas, were wearing colorful African outfits and singing:

> *"La plena viene de Ponce.*
> "The *plena* comes from Ponce.
>
> *¡Y viene del Barrio de San Antón!"*
> And it comes from San Antón!"

Mami was brave! In front of Abuelita, she came out to the street to hug Doña Monse and Don Toño, who were dancing a *plena* by a float decorated with bright red hibiscus and purple *trinitarias*.

I didn't look back to see Abuelita's reaction. Because, under an arch of *trinitarias* on the float, stood Ana.

As Ana moved to wave at people, the sequins on the leaves that gathered up the skirt moved as if a gentle breeze had touched them. The *níspero*-seed beads on the creamy-colored tulle sparkled along with Ana's *níspero* eyes.

A street lamp shined down on her float, and I felt as if in the shade of a *níspero* tree.

"Ana! Ana!" I cried, jumping up and down for her to see me.

"Ana!" Marisol called too.

"Ana!" the newspaper photographers around her float also called.

But Ana's eyes turned to me. She placed both hands on her mouth and blew me a kiss. I blew her one back.

The dimpled smile on her face got as big as the crescent moon. *Bigger* than the moon.

And I knew exactly how she felt.

Exactly. Because I also felt that way.